FULL MAMABEAR

NINA M WILDE

Full Mamabear

By Nina M. Wilde

COPYRIGHT

Disclaimer: Even though this book is written in British English, in Birmingham generally they use mom and not mum.

Copyright 2019 Nina M. Wilde. No part of this book may be copied or reproduced. All rights reserved. For translation or film rights please contact the author.

FROM THE AUTHOR

You can follow me on social media:

On Instagram I am @ninamwilde
And Facebook I am @fullmamabear

Or go to www.ninamwilde.com to sign up for my newsletter, where you can receive free content and learn about my new releases.

FORUMFRIENDS MOMS' GROUP

Jaime right - 22nd July - 19:33

Hi everyone, welcome to our ForumFriends moms' group. I decided to set this up after all the drama with the original group and Kayleigh; I felt like a smaller one would be nicer, and we could get to know each other a bit easier. If you're happy to, please introduce yourself below. I'll start. I'm Jaime, I'm 34 and a lawyer from Birmingham. I mostly just do wills and probate. My husband is Olly and my little girl is called River, she's seven weeks old today.

Erin Schellenger - 22nd July - 19:36

Let's not talk about Kayleigh, shall we? Lol. I'm Erin, 38, originally from Milwaukee. I moved to the UK to go to uni, met my husband Ben, and we bought a crumbly old cottage in the Cotswolds. I run a vlog about being a confused American in the UK, it's called 'What The Heck Is Squash Anyway?' check me out on YouTube! My baby is Sam, and he'll be 6 weeks old tomorrow.

Carys Honeyman - 22nd July - 19:37

I'm Carys, from Wrexham. I live with my fiancé Amy, and our little boy Dylan, 7 weeks old yesterday. I'm a first-time mum and I work as a dental hygienist for a private clinic.

Kelly Vaughan - 22nd July - 19:39
Kelly here. SAHM. Sort of single. Rosie was born on 4th June. I have three older kids, Tyler (10), Aiden (7), and Toby (4). I can stop now I have my girl lol. I live in Derby. I've always dreamed of running my own hotel.

Molly Cheung - 22nd July - 19:44
I'm Molly, I live with my husband in Weston-super-Mare, I'm also a SAHM. Jasper is 5 weeks old, and I have toddler twins, Dexter and Alexia. If you don't already know, I'm almost completely blind, have been since birth. I'm a massive book nerd, though for obvious reasons I prefer audio books. I especially love anything by Audrey Parlour.

Jeanie Gillespie - 22nd July - 19:48
Hello everyone, I'm Jeanie. I'm 46. Mae will be 5 weeks tomorrow, which means I'm what they call a 'geriatric mother' yay. I have a teenage daughter, Maddison, and we live in Cambridge. Maddison and Mae have the same dad, but we don't really speak much. I work in an art supplies shop and I fucking hate it, currently trying to figure out a way to not go back next year.

Marie Sparks - 22nd July - 20:25
So glad you set this group up, I felt lost in the other one. I'm Marie, I'm 25 and a primary school teacher in Lincoln. I'm a first-time mum and live with my husband, Rob. Looking forward to getting to know you all a bit more closely.

Ruchi Kapoor - 22nd July - 20:31
Hello everyone. I'm Ruchi, I live in London with my husband,

and our little boy. I run my own cake decorating business from my garden kitchen. I love anything to do with baking and cooking.

Georgia Kerr - 22nd July - 20:37

Great idea Jaime, I never felt involved in the other group. I'm Georgia, I'm 17, from Edinburgh. I'm just finishing my final year of college and then hopefully going to uni in Sept. I live with my boyfriend and our little boy, Hunter, who is 4 weeks old.

Natalie Dixon - 22nd July – 22:59

Hi everyone, sorry for the delay. I'm Natalie, I live in signal trap Cornwall with my daughter Riley, 6 weeks, and my mum, who is poorly, and whom I care for full time. I'm a SAHM, and occasional dog walker. Really excited to get to know you all better.

CHAPTER ONE

Of all the offices at Caine Reynolds, Clive's was the biggest, and probably the least personalised. Just a single framed photograph of himself on the course with some, probably famous, golfer. No plants or trinkets or holiday souvenirs like the other fee-earners had, and no photos of his kids. If I remembered correctly, he has two grown-up sons, though I think they had both moved away to Australia or New Zealand or something.

He had said to meet him in his office at 8 a.m. When I last glanced at the clock, it read 8:40. *Urgh*. His office was immaculate, but boring AF. There was nothing there to keep me mentally occupied. At all. I had read and reread the same bloody Post-it on the side of his monitor at least a million times: 'Final balance due Sat, pick up from Fri 13th'. I was desperate to look at my phone, to scroll through the ForumFriends moms' group I admined, though I knew there probably wouldn't be any new posts from this morning, but I resisted. I had been caught way too many times on my phone at work, especially in the run-up to my mat leave. How would that look on my first shift back?

At some point during the forty minutes I had been waiting here, my fingers had found, and settled on, a tiny nick in the vinyl on the corner of Clive's once relatively pristine white desk. As acting partner of the Birmingham branch, he could have chosen any desk he liked. I remember flicking through the office supplies catalogues when I first started eight or so years ago and daydreaming about which statement pieces I would select when I made partner one day. It's the slightly more grown-up equivalent of browsing the Argos catalogue as a child, cutting out lamps and swing-sets, and creating a 'future home' mood board. Personally, I would have chosen this lovely mahogany desk from page 58 of the 'Better Office' supplies book – yeah, it's expensive and showy, but it's important. Instead, he opted for an uninspiring, flimsy sheet of particle board covered with a shiny, plastic 'wood-effect' sticker. I don't get it – it's not even his money he's spending.

However, by the time my consciousness finally caught up with me, I had picked away at the once teeny-tiny nick in the vinyl until it was roughly the size of my c-section scar.

Oh shit.

The area of exposed chipboard was approximately six inches long and an inch high, and the carpet around the table leg looked as though it was suffering from very bad dandruff. I flashed the clock another quick look. Hopefully I would have time to fix this before Clive arrived. Would he notice, though, or care? He didn't seem to spend much time in this room.

I'd better try to fix it, or hide it, at the very least. I snapped a quick picture of the damage with my phone – I know, I didn't want to get my phone out, but I couldn't figure this one out on my own – and I uploaded it to the moms' group. One of them would surely have the answer?

Jaime Wright - 2nd March - 08:42
Help, please! It's my first day back at work and I've just done this to my boss's desk without realising. How can I fix it?!

Responses came almost immediately.

Jeanie Gillespie - 2nd March - 08:43
Oh no hun! How did you manage that? Maybe try covering it with some Tipp-Ex? Good luck on the rest of your first day back. xx

Kelly Vaughan - 2nd March - 08:44
LMAO babes. Just peel the whole desk off to match and maybe he won't notice.

Molly Cheung - 2nd March - 08:45
I can't believe you're back to work already, it's flown. Can you find something to stick over it?

Kelly Vaughan - 2nd March - 08:46
Or you could turn the whole desk around? So the shitty patch is facing the other way?

Hiding it seemed the most sensible and rapidly achievable solution, but what to use…? I rummaged through the desk drawers, hoping to find some correction fluid or something similar. In the middle drawer, among standard stationary debris, and underneath a NSFW soft-core magazine, I found a small bottle of Tipp-Ex, possibly dating back to the 90s. I took it from the drawer and removed the cap. The lid was stiff and gunked together, and the contents were goopy – though not completely dried out – so I pasted a generous layer onto the bare chipboard. It smelled like a chemical fish, and the texture resembled a homemade face mask I once made using 'everyday' shit you find in the kitchen, including porridge oats, baking soda, and a £30 jar of honey.

Oh bugger. That made it worse.

I ripped a piece of printer paper into thin strips and pushed them onto the porridge patch. Where the still-wet correction fluid stuck to the paper, it turned see-through, like little spots of grease.

Shit, shit, shit.

It was a million times worse than if I had done nothing at all but left a bare patch on the desk. I should have just ignored it and pretended I didn't know it was there – maybe I still could. Though, to be honest, if he wasn't so late, I wouldn't have fucked it up in the first place.

In a last-ditch attempt, I grabbed some white Blu Tack and tried to smush it into the bigger craters, shaping it with my fingertips, and leaving dirty imprints along the way.

Wow, my hands were filthy! I examined my fingernails and then my handiwork. It was difficult to tell which of the two was the most shameful.

It would have to do. I looked at the clock again – 8:56 a.m., where is he? I took out my phone, snapped another picture and uploaded it to the moms' group with the caption "nailed it" and eight lopsided laughing emojis.

"On your phone again?! You've only just got back!

Some things never bloody change, do they?"

Leaping from my chair, I threw my phone back into my open handbag. Clive had just entered his office. He walked around the desk, took a seat in his high-backed chair, and indicated that I should sit back down too. He did not appear to have noticed the bodged desk corner. Thank God.

"How's the wee baby? What's his name again?"

"Her name. She's a girl. She's called River. She's doing really well, thank you," I said, rather more formally than I intended.

"That's an interesting name," said Clive. He looked as though he had just swallowed a fly.

And that was all that was said on the matter of my baby, and the reason that I had been off work for the best part of a year.

He slapped his thighs like he was playing a drumbeat. "You back full time? Or part time?"

"Part time. I'm doing four half days per week for four weeks and then HR are going discuss my flexible return." Whatever that means.

Clive was silent for a few moments. Often, it was difficult to tell whether he was paying attention at all, due to his very slight boss eye. It was only a very subtle outwards turn, but enough that you occasionally need to check behind yourself when in conversation with him, just to make sure he hadn't actually been looking at someone else all along. I knew that we were alone in his office, yet the urge to double-check behind me was so strong I had to squint, so that his features became blurred.

"Have you signed your return-to-work paperwork yet?" he asked, possibly to me, possibly to the door.

"No, Rachel said that you would get the forms for me to sign."

"Why would I have them?!" He shrugged. He began demonstrably opening his desk drawers and lifting up papers as if to show me that he wasn't hiding them anywhere. "I'll have Rachel get them for you. In the meantime, your licences have expired because you've missed so much work—"

"I've been on matern—" I began in defence, but Clive just carried on talking as though I hadn't spoken.

"So you can't take on any real clients yet. You'll have to do some more training to get you up to date, and you'll have to resit your licence exams. I'll speak with head office and see if they can forward your training schedule. I'll make a note." He heaved a loaded A4 black diary onto the desk, but neither attempted to open it to the correct date, nor make a note, like he just said he would.

"Do you have any idea when that might be?" I said, wondering why, when Clive had known for months the exact date of my return, hadn't he already organised my training so that I could slip seamlessly back into my old role. I didn't voice any of this aloud, though.

He shrugged his shoulders. "No, sorry. A week, maybe two. For the meantime, you can shadow Ryan."

"Ryan?! Ryan Burgess? But... Ryan is just a legal executive. He's two pay grades below me."

And he wears shorts to client meetings for crying out loud.

Clive kissed his teeth at me. I knew it was the use of the word 'just'. I honestly didn't mean to say it; it was a slip of the tongue. "Well, he passed his training while you were off, and he's a fully qualified solicitor now."

I took a deep breath, maybe a softer approach would be better. "But, why Ryan?"

Clive sighed. I braced myself. I was about to get an earful of exactly why Ryan.

"I know he might not be everyone's cup of tea, but he does know his place in this company," he began. "He's very talented, and not afraid to push for more. And he has a 'way' with the clients, especially the ladies." (Barf) "No, I think shadowing Ryan will be the best option to ease you back into work. You could learn a lot from him, Jaime. And I shouldn't be saying this, but, we – the partners I mean – have got something great planned for him at the end of the month."

I could not manage to form coherent thoughts. My eyes darted left and right between Clive's good, and not so good, eyes. Was it possible that I would just have to sit around and wait for someone to put through the necessary paperwork so that I could do my job again? Surely you didn't *need* to be qualified to write wills. And to shadow Ryan Burgess of all people. A man that once 'accidentally' sent dick pics to a recently widowed client.

"Don't look so pissed," said Clive, reading my expression. "You're only working four hours a day." He looked at the clock on the wall. "It's already half-past nine, you've only got another two and a half hours. And don't forget *we're* still paying you full-time wages." He raised his eyebrows and, with a churlish flick of his head towards the door, he dismissed me from his office.

So that's how it is.

I bent forward and picked up my handbag. As I brought the open bag level to the desk, Clive must have caught sight of the funnel attachment and bulbous handle of my breast-pump inside.

"And you can't do that here," he said, looking at the pump as if it was a dead rat.

"Do what?" I knew exactly what he was referring to but I needed him to say it out loud just to be sure.

"You can't express milk in this building." His neck was

beginning to flush red in patches. He shook his head. "There's nowhere you can do it safely. I'd have to do a risk assessment, and... I just don't have the time. Plus, you don't get any paid breaks when you're only working a four hour shift."

I sucked my teeth back at him. "Right. Thank you." I allowed myself one last look at the bodged porridge desk corner and suddenly felt very pleased.

Erin Schellenger - 2nd March - 11:40
Can he even do that? Is that legal? Surely they HAVE to let you express somewhere?

Jaime Wright - 2nd March - 11:42
Sadly, it's not a legal requirement for an employer to provide you with anywhere to express. I had no choice I had to do it on the loo.

Molly Cheung - 2nd March - 11:43
That's awful hun. Isn't it discrimination?

Jaime Wright - 2nd March - 11:44
He's the managing partner at this branch, he's basically the top lawyer here. He knows exactly what he's doing, and he's not about to do anything that would get him into any legal trouble.

Marie Sparks - 2nd March - 11:45
That sucks. I'm so sorry.

. . .

I had already resigned the rest of my first shift back to pissing about on my phone. I had gotten completely bored of 'shadowing' Ryan, who, thirty minutes previously, had declared that he was "off for a dump" and had not yet returned to his desk.

I'd once had one of the tiny offices lining the front of the building, but had discovered upon returning that it was being used as storage space for Property. If I leant back far enough in my chair I could see some sunlight triumphantly trying to pierce its way through the gaps in the many stacks of boxes. I guess, at some point, that I will probably get my office back, maybe when I have my licenses renewed and I get my own clients again. There was a nice desk underneath all those deeds, a charming, yet inexpensive, number from page 75; not quite partner-level grand, but it had a quirky mid-century repro style to it. Hopefully someone from admin will come and clear the things off it. For the time being, I had been forced to share a desk with 'Him' in the common office space with the paralegals, underwriters, and the PAs. A space informally known to everyone as The Chamber. Not that I really mind, but I'd worked bloody hard for that tiny office.

"You didn't come and see me." The empty space in Ryan's chair was filled with a familiar and welcoming accent, an odd sort of Irish tinged with Brummie.

I turned to look at her, smiling, but I hid my face with my hands. "I'm sorry, I've just had the worst first day back ever."

Niamh worked in Family, on the other side of the sixth floor. She was the only person I considered a friend IRL, i.e. not in the moms' group on my phone. She didn't ask me why I'd had such a terrible start to my day, and I didn't bother to elaborate. I knew that she would understand; she had worked here as long as I had, she's got kids, and has been on, and returned from, maternity leave. She hugged me and gave me a kiss on the top of my head.

"Oh hun, you could try washing your hair once in a while."

I punched her in the arm. "It'll be okay when I get all of my training back up to date," I said, more to console myself than to Niamh.

"Not all law firms are as shitty as this one. Well, actually, it's probably just this branch to be fair. I heard that the Worcester one is OK. Maybe we could transfer together?" she said, stroking my hair. "Or…" Her eyes grew wide, like she'd just had a brilliant idea, though I knew she was playacting. "We could just fuck it all off and start our own firm?"

I laughed. A recurrent joke between the two of us, occasionally surfacing into conversation, usually after a few proseccos.

A few people looked up from their desks in minor, feigned interest.

"I mean, who's not going to hire a solicitor from Goode and Wright? Am I right? Sounds better than Caine Reynolds anyway."

"It could be Wright and Goode?"

"Pfft whatever," said Niamh, her eyes wrinkling as she smiled. "Anyway, I brought this for you." She pushed a box towards me that I hadn't noticed before. It was an old toner box, with a white sticky label on the front that said 'shit saved from Jaime's office'.

"Aw, thanks," I said. I peered inside.

There was a photo frame with a picture of my mom, dad, sister and me from when we went to Disneyland Paris, or as it was known at the time: EuroDisney. My dad: lanky and white, my mom: short and black, my sister and I: the perfect blend of their two skin tones, standing between them. We all look miserable as sin, but I swear it was one of my happiest memories. In the box there was also a 'crying emoji' plush that Niamh's son won from a grabber when we all went to Blackpool together. He gave it to me as a gift because he had won all the emoji plushes and said that this one would be most suitable for my desk at work. It was either the crying one, or the poo one – I'd opted for the crying one. A caricature drawing of Olly and I from our wedding in Vegas. Classy, but we hadn't really had time to arrange a photographer. And lastly, there was a napkin from Nandos that Niamh had drawn a picture of a ticket on with the words 'outta here' in the middle. She gave it to me when she first told me of her ludicrous idea about starting our own firm. I don't know why I kept this really; it still has bits of chicken grease on it. It's kind of gross actually.

Anyway, it was just a silly daydream. I'm a solicitor, not a businesswoman. Where would we even start? I wrote wills, not business things.

No pub after work for me these days; I still had to pick up River from nursery at 12:30, BabySwim classes at 1:00, Bounce and Sing at the library at 2:30, and to top it off we only had Ella's pouches and Imodium at home to eat, so I would need to make a quick pit stop at the supermarket if we wanted something more substantial than strawberry sauce and constipation for tea.

I pulled into Tesco carpark at roughly 3:30, just in time for the deluge of school-run-moms and their offspring.

I drummed my fingers against the steering wheel and contemplated the acute shitstorm that was today. To add to my wonderful first shift back, River had also taken an enormous crap in the pool at BabySwim, forcing us to miss the second half of the £15, 30-minute session. And at Bounce and Sing, the awful woman that had stood in when the kindly librarian was on holiday, kept referring to River as 'he', and frequently passed comment on how small he was for his age and how it was probably because he was still being breastfed, and at that age he really ought to be eating proper food like fish fingers and chips – or have I tried melting a Rusk into a bottle of milk… and I really ought to dress her in more pink if I didn't want people to think she was a boy.

Ah fuck off Carol, you nosey bitch.

There were no parking spaces anywhere.

Then, like the cherry on top of the whipped cream on top of the cake, it began to rain. Like soaked-to-the-bone-in-an-instant, pissing rain.

Fantastic.

I drove up and down the lanes in the car park hoping to find an appropriate space and eventually spotted one next to the disabled bays – but I was catfished by a KA. *Oh FFS*! Then Mr Blue Sky came on the radio. I hate that song. I smashed the dashboard and turned it off, preferring to listen to the robotic whish-whish of the wind-screen wipers.

After her giant shit earlier, River was now dozing happily in her car seat. It would make the shop easier, maybe even enjoyable, if I could just pop the whole seat into one of those trollies with the basket bit on the top, and do the whole shop with her napping. *Hmm, fifteen minutes of peace: what a treat.* Maybe I would even look for some new slippers.

There!

Perfect! A parent-and-child space was opening up not far from where we were, and what's more, it was right next to the sheltered walkway so River and I wouldn't get too wet on our way into the shop. I put my indicator on and waited for the current occupant, a black Honda, to leave. The man driver smiled and gave me a half-wave as he drove out of the space. His kids in the back seat looked as though they were having a rave.

I was mere feet away from pulling into the space, when a bastard silver BMW X5 with a personalised number plate sped out of nowhere and slipped between the white lines, swiping the spot right from under my nose.

"Fuck's sake," I muttered aloud. "I had my fucking indicator on."

An older couple then exited the car. Without a single glance at me in my C4 Picasso, the man locked his car over his shoulder with the key fob. No kids in sight.

I wound down the window. "Oi, mate!" I said, in what I thought was an unwarranted polite voice. "That space is for people with kids."

The woman, whose face remained completely static (probably fillers) yelled back. "Never had none of these spaces when we was younger. You can just walk like we had to."

The pair laughed loudly together like she had told a hilarious joke.

They did not stop walking, so when the man yelled to me, it was barely audible over the driving rain. "If you don't want to walk with your kids in the rain then maybe you shouldn't've had kids!"

I knew there was no way he would hear my response, and that's probably why I yelled out the way I did. "What brilliant advice, mate. Thank you! Maybe I'll go back in time and remember my pill that day. You shitbag wankers!" It didn't really make sense, but it made me feel fleetingly better.

Oh crap, I'd forgotten about River in the back. She stirred and then drifted back to sleep.

The man shrugged his shoulders and cupped his hand over his ear, and still grinning broadly, the couple continued the last twenty feet into the shop under the lovely dry walkway.

Slightly shaking, I now had to choose between parking round the back and getting piss-soaked on the way to the shop, or parking near the entrance but having to wake River. The narrow spaces meant that I wouldn't be able to open the doors wide enough take the whole car seat out. I chose the shorter route near the entrance.

There were no trollies. *Fucking brilliant.* I would've bet anything those BMW wankers took the last one.

Having been torn from her cosy slumber, River began screaming her adorable little head off. Her face became beetroot red, she sounded like a Mandrake. People were avoiding us in the supermarket, choosing different aisles if they could, or else tutting and shaking their heads from a distance.

I couldn't quite figure out how to carry a screaming baby and a shopping basket at the same time, so I abandoned the stupid basket by the magazine aisle, kicking it into a display of Mothering Sunday cards. How ironic. I would have to carry everything I needed to buy in my free arm. I walked straight past the slippers without a second glance.

I was halfway round the store, in the tinned goods section, when I almost ran headfirst into Mr. and Mrs. BMW. Did they recognise me? I stood stock-still, my face burning, and attempted to stare them down. They didn't move. I wanted to challenge them, ask them why they were such jerks, and if they were happy now that my baby was audibly assaulting everyone in the vicinity – but I could only manage a slightly affronted grimace.

I imagined lobbing a can of baked beans right into their stupid faces. The satisfying crunchy thwack the tin would make against that woman's plasticky face, and that man's ridiculous, 80s-snooker-player moustache.

Suddenly, and simultaneously, the couple's eyes flashed. Maybe they remembered who I was: that angry mom from the car park with her screaming child. Or maybe they thought that I would start something. It was a pretty terrifying grimace to be fair. They turned on the spot and hobbled away from me, through the angular trolley maze.

Yeah, you run.

With River still screaming – why won't that child shut up? – I abandoned all plans to gather actual ingredients and hastened to the wine section and then the chocolate aisle. After a few perilous seconds where I grappled to balance my wailing flesh-sack – I mean beautiful baby – the Cabernet Sauvignon, and the family-sized bag of Revels, I bolted to the check-out.

I made eye contact with no one, keeping my head down, but the tsk-tsks still followed me around the shop.

I paid for the chocolate and wine, spilling coins all over the bag-packing area and the poor cashier. Was it possible that he felt sorry for me? I wasn't sure; I couldn't bear to look at him for more than a nanosecond, or anyone else, and left the shop as quickly as humanly possible.

As I drove past the enormous silver car that stole my parking space, I imagined what would have happened if I'd grabbed the trolley from the BMW Wankers and smashed it into the wall of tins beside them, raining an avalanche of spaghetti hoops and kidney beans, and maybe even a couple of smashed jars of Dolmio upon them, until they were completely buried and the only thing remaining amid the mountain of cans was a single, solitary hand clasping at the air.

I ripped opened the 'more to share' bag of Revels, gave one huge scoffing laugh, and tipped its entire contents into my mouth. Chocolate pieces flew out and showered the dashboard, my lap, and the footwells.

"How was it, babe?" said Olly, walking into the kitchen that evening. He caught sight of me and dropped his messenger bag to the floor. I was slumped at the breakfast bar drinking red wine straight out of the bottle – probably not a great sight. "Oh no. That bad?"

"I literally had the worst day ever."

He listened while I told him everything that had happened that day. He had long since learnt not to make what he thought of as helpful suggestions to improve my situation, but instead, to appease me by correctly gasping, growling, and naw-ing where necessary during my story. Boy did good. Also sometimes patting my hair helped, and food too. Food always helped.

"That's it, we're getting takeaway," he said, when I had finished telling him about the floor of our family car which was now littered with slightly melted chocolates. Technically it was my car anyway; it was in my name, and Oliver's two-seater beast was definitely not baby-friendly, but I still felt a twang of guilt about the carpets, and the lost Revels. Hopefully they were all the chocolate raisin ones. *Bleurgh*.

The sacrificial lamb pasanda, chicken tikka masala, rice, naans and assortment of 'oh we've never tried this before, hope it's not okra again' had been ordered from Just Eat and would be with us in 45 minutes. About ten seconds later we got an email to say it would be with us in 55 minutes.

The food and booze lifted my spirits considerably. Oliver provided entertainment by doing his best Ryan impressions. These involved standing on his tip toes and saying sexist things in a sluggish voice, such as "Oi Jaime, go make me a sandwich," and, "You'd look better if your tits were hanging out of your top, love," all while bumping into things in the kitchen. It was stupid and hilarious, and by the time we went to bed that evening we were wheezy from laughing. Mostly at the knowledge that I would be getting paid a full-time wage to sit at a – usually unoccupied – desk, pissing about on ForumFriends all day.

Before bed I listened at the crack to River's bedroom door for her purring little snores, just to make sure she was still alive. There are always a few terrifying seconds where you suddenly remember you have a baby, and in those exact moments you are convinced that they have stopped breathing. She was fine; sounded a bit snotty maybe – probably all the crying she did at Tesco. At least I had succeeded in motherhood for another day... sort of.

I tiptoed back across the landing to the bathroom, hopping over that one wobbly floorboard which just so happened to sit right over the water pipes, and gently pulled the light cord. I had little energy to brush my teeth or take my make-up off, but I still did both, because once a magazine article said that it was life or death level important to do it, though I couldn't remember what the consequences would be if I forgot.

I stared into the mirror as I brushed my teeth. All I could see were two enormous black totes that were my eyebags, and my line of baby hairs across the top of my forehead; nice to see my hair was finally starting to grow back. Post partum hair loss: what a pleasant surprise for the unsuspecting first-time mom. I stared so hard that the bathroom around me dissolved into blackness; even my hair eventually disappeared and only two droopy, brown eyes stared back. Was it even normal that my brain did this? I wondered if other people get this too.

I shook away the tunnel vision, spat out the toothpaste froth, and crept back over the landing and into bed. Oliver was already asleep, facing the wall. He too was snoring, though somewhat less adorably than his daughter.

After snuggling into the blankets and plugging my phone into the charger, I chose not to go to sleep right away. These were my last few moments of peace, so I would spend them checking my ForumFriends page – more specifically for the moms' group that I ran. There were a few new posts since the last time I looked, one about car seats, another about nappy rash, and a few photos of some of the other babies who were all roughly the same age as River. It was a typical online moms' group – but it was *my* moms' group.

Diligently, I went through each of the photos and the posts, and 'heart-reacted' or sometimes 'sad-face-reacted' where appropriate. It was my job, my role, as admin of the group, but also as a friend.

In real life I am largely friendless. In school I never belonged to any of the cliques, and in uni I chose to live with my Dad instead of staying at the dorms like most of the other law students. Even at work, nobody but Niamh got me, understood my jokes. I pictured the other moms from the group, sitting in the dark, with blue faces and phone halos just like me; each with their – hopefully sleeping – babies, and their brilliant advice re sore bums and breastfeeding and baby-led weaning. They understood my jokes, especially the ones about my mother-in-law. I was myself in this group. They were my clique.

CHAPTER TWO

My wake-up call came, predictably, at 5am. This time, River had poonamied through her darling bunny-rabbit sleeping bag and had executed flawless corner to corner coverage of her cotbed mattress. I hosed down the baby in the shower and, still clutching my naked child, I one-handedly stripped the bedding, bundled it into a neat little poo-parcel and posted it in the washing machine with double the amount of detergent powder I would normally use. Fun fact: most of my first nine months of parenting has been learning how to do everything using only one arm.

I made a cup of black coffee that I would inevitably forget about until it was cold, took River into the living room, and put the telly onto the CBeebies' holding screen, waiting for Mr Tumble, or some other gravely happy behemoth to further ruin my morning.

Oliver slept soundly throughout. Because he had work later that day, but also because it was just another one of those things that I never asked for help with, even though I knew he would. He was good like that.

At 7:30 a.m., I dropped River to nursery and drove across town to the office. There was a lot of traffic, even for rush hour Birmingham. Before River, I would have typically considered anything later than fifteen minutes early to be inexcusably tardy. The dashboard clock was now reading 7:55. My stomach churned. I was going to be late on my second day back to work. And not just Jaime late, but real-late late.

I arrived at the building at 7:59 and repeatedly punched the up button on the lifts, hopping up and down as I waited for the doors to open. Paul, the doorman, probably thought I needed a wee. I could just take the stairs – it might be faster.

The doors opened with an absolving ping.

"Good morning, Jamie." A short woman, with curly grey hair walked into the building and followed me into the lift. "Lovely to see you back. How's motherhood treating you?"

I was ready for the question. In fact, every mother is. The answer is already prepared, because there is only one acceptable response, or at least only one that people want to hear.

"Amazing. Thank you. It's everything I ever dreamed it would be." I gave a robotic smile. "Please excuse the smell, I got shat on this morning," I added.

"How are you finding being back at work?" asked Frances, brushing over my answer with a forced laugh. The doors closed and she pressed the number six button.

I faltered. "Uh..." This was a question for which I did not have an answer prepared. Disappointed? Undervalued? Annoyed? Maybe even angry? That was the truth. Perhaps, and I was just realising this, that most of all I was looking forward to having actual conversations with actual adults, and instead I've ended up being paired with an overgrown child having no conversations whatsoever and doing absolutely fuck-all all day. No, that was bad, but the biggest disappointment of my first day back was feeling totally and utterly useless, unproductive, not needed, and not helpful to anybody. I've always been a doer – I needed to be doing something.

Frances laughed at my silent non-response and gave a sympathetic tilt of her head. "You know I think you might just be in the wrong place in this company," she said.

"Yeah Niamh said the same, that maybe we ought to go to Worcester."

"Ooh no, you don't want to go to Worcester, bunch of morons there. No, no, I'm talking about moving departments. I know what it's like working for Clive. Got the T-shirt and all that. I have to admit it's not that much fun, but not all of the offices here are so…" She looked around the lift as if the right word might be written on the mirrored walls. "…So blokey. You could come work on the other side of the office, away from the lads? Come work in Family."

There was something kind of appealing about transferring to Family, not least because I would be working directly with Niamh.

"Are there any positions in Family at the moment?" I asked.

"Um, no." Frances sighed. "Buuuut, *I'm* retiring at the end of the month, and they haven't decided on my replacement yet."

Did she just wink at me?

We reached the sixth floor, the doors pinged open again and we both got out of the lift, neither of us taking our gaze away from the other.

"But you're a partner," I said, almost tripping up on the bottom of the doors.

"Yes…" Frances raised her eyebrows.

What did she mean? Did Frances want to put me forward for the partner position? It certainly sounded that way, but nobody in their right mind would make me a partner yet – surely? I'd only just come back from maternity leave and still had all my return-to-work training to complete. Sure, I'd dreamt of making partner at Caine Reynolds since I first started, and it would be a huge bonus that I wouldn't be in Wills and Probate any more with Clive and Ryan. Maybe I'd even get my 'objection your honour' dream come true after all.

I checked over my shoulder, just to make sure Clive wasn't around – we were alone in the tiny foyer. "Clive would never allow it; he absolutely hates me. And I don't have any experience in Family. I'm not sure if Niamh would think it was a good idea either, really." *Why was I trying to push this opportunity away?*

"Why not?" said Frances, frowning.

"I'm too emotional. She doesn't think I can handle Family. I cried at the mayonnaise commercial."

"Well that was a sad— Wait, the mayonnaise one? The one with the pig in the duffle-coat?"

"Honestly, don't even get me thinking about it," I said fanning myself with one hand.

Still frowning, Frances said, "Well it's not Clive you'd need to worry about anyway. You'd need the approval of all the other partners."

Well that'll never happen then. "How many are there again?"

"Oh, only eighteen, not including me."

"Right… I don't even think they know I exist."

"Of course they do Jaime, don't be so silly. You've only been away for ten… eleven months. You just need to do something to remind them that you exist. Something to impress them. Capture their attention. You're a very good lawyer, I don't need to remind you that. I would just hate to see your talents wasted in the Chamber. Not that there's anything wrong with Wills and Probate of course, it's just that… you should be somewhere where you can put your skills to better use. To do some good in the world, you know?"

She couldn't know it, but she was saying exactly the right things to trigger my daydream reflexes: "Be useful, do some good". It's exactly why I studied law in the first place. Well, that and my mom told my sister and me to.

"What the fuck Jaime, you're three minutes and forty-five seconds late." Niamh appeared in the entrance of the East side offices clutching a stack of manila files and tapping her wrist.

"Have a think anyway," said Frances. This time she definitely winked at me. "Morning Niamh." Then she disappeared around the same corner Niamh had come from.

"Think about what?" said Niamh, once Frances was out of earshot.

"Fran told me that she's retiring at the end of the month and seems to think I might be in with a shot for partner."

Niamh let out a derisive snort of laughter.

The speed and readiness with which she dismissed the suggestion stung. I turned on the spot and walked into the Chamber and up to Ryan's empty desk. Of course this would be her response; never one to dance around the truth, but nevertheless it still made me feel shitty. Wasn't I good enough to work in Family? Clive always spoke about the Family lawyers as if they were a bit soft, a bit too bohemian, and definitely too liberal.

"Oh, I didn't mean it like that," said Niamh, chasing

after me. "It's just that... well, one, you've only just got back from maternity leave, and, in the history of the company, I've never known anyone to be promoted – especially to partner – after they just get back from maternity leave. Two, you hate this job. Three, it's a horrible, bigoted company and nobody wants to work here, period. Why do you think Fran is retiring early? And... wait what number am I up to?"

"Four."

"And four—"

"You don't think I'm emotionally strong enough?"

"Noooooo," she said. There was a 'but' coming. "We do deal with a lot of domestic abuse cases, but that's not what I was going to say."

"What were you going to say, then?"

She sighed. "Your main problem, Jaime, is that you never think things through properly."

I frowned at her.

"You just rush into things without ever really thinking about it. You're too impulsive, and when you do make plans, well they... they never work out."

That's just another way to say that my plans are always shit.

She pursed her lips. "OK, so, like, you got married in Vegas, drunk; you got pregnant because you went camping and left your pill at home..."

"I'm failing to see how these things haven't worked out," I said, folding my arms. "I've got a great husband and a beautiful little girl."

"OK maybe those are bad examples. But look, you came back to work and picked all the vinyl off Clive's desk without thinking."

"Yeah..."

"And now you want to come and work in Family without even really knowing anything about it."

"I just want to do actual, proper work and be taken seriously again. Fuck knows how long I'll have to 'shadow' Ryan." I did air quotes. "I'm an associate solicitor and all I've done so far since getting back to work is order some more breastmilk bags off eBay and looked at cake ideas on Pinterest for River's first birthday."

"I'm sorry, hun."

"I think I'm going to go for a buttercream lion design, in case you were wondering."

"That sounds lovely. Look I'm sorry th—"

A thought suddenly occurred to me. "Oh my god!I''m so sorry. I didn't think that *you* might want the position. Naturally you'd be a better candidate than me. Shit, no wonder you don't want me to do it, how insensitive."

"Actually, I don't want it. They haven't asked me, and even if they did, I would turn it down."

"They haven't asked you? Why? Niamh, you'd be perfect for it. Why would you turn it down?"

Niamh glanced around the room and pursed her lips together. "Haven't you ever noticed how few women make partner here? Like, not just here in the Birmingham branch, but across the whole company. They just don't pick women for the top positions... especially not ones of child-bearing age."

"What about Fran? She's a woman."

"She told me that she only made partner once she went through menopause."

"Really? That's awful."

"Yep, once they'd stopped looking at her as a liability, or an object, all her dreams came true." She shrugged, as if to say "What can you do about it?"

"Well, things have to move forward at some point.

They can't just keep hiring dudes all the time, especially when some of us are more qualified for the position than others."

Ryan's face swam before my eyes.

After a few moments Niamh sighed and said, "Sorry hun, I didn't want to say anything yet because you've only just got back, but... I've been looking at jobs in other firms."

There was a sharp pain in my stomach, as if somebody had punched me. It was kind of like the feeling you get when you know you've been short-changed but it's too late to do anything about.

"Nooooooo! You can't go. I'll have no one for company except..." I looked down at Ryan's empty chair. "He makes fart noises every time I sit down." My throat began to feel tight.

"Well, the offer to set up a practice of our own is still there. I mean, it'll be the most difficult thing we've ever done – after raising our babies obviously – but can you imagine how amazing it would be? Nobody to tell us what to do, or wear, and we can focus on the areas of law that appeal the most. Olly earns enough to support you both, right? So does Mike, until we can get the company off the ground..."

It *was* a really cool idea. But it would never happen. I just could never see myself having enough resolve to branch out on my own. I'm a terrible decision-maker as it is. I shook the thought from my head. I couldn't just gamble everything I've worked towards for a pipe dream. And besides, Niamh has already told me how awful my plans always turn out.

"If I can get partner here; I'll be your boss and I won't let you leave." I winked.

Niamh gave a weak smile in reply. "In that case, you'd

better think of something really fucking awesome to grab the other partners' attention."

"Right...on it," I said. I walked around the desk, drumming my fingers across my mouth. *Hmm*. I pulled out Ryan's chair, and there, on the seat, was a three-inch ream of papers bound with an elastic band and labelled with a sticky yellow note on the top.

Jaime, I need x2 copies of this. Ta, R.

"Fuck my life." I thumbed through the papers and let out a long, low grunt.

"Don't do it, hun. You're not his fucking PA."

I cast my eyes around the room. Half of the desks were still vacant, and everyone else was clearly pretending they couldn't hear us.

"It's fine, whatever. Come on, I'll follow you to your desk."

"I can't do it today I'm afraid," said Lauren, when I brought over the stack of photocopying to the admin office. "I know ordinarily you would just fill out one of those slips, and we'd do it for you, but we're swamped today. Just don't have any time. We're organising the annual Caine Reynolds' Awards Presentations. It's less than two weeks away!"

"Ah the CRAPs." I nodded. "I totally forgot about those. No matter, I can do it. I've got absolutely nothing else to do anyway. I think I remember how it works."

I stood next to the photocopier and bit my lip. Probably you just press this green button here... The machine whirred into life, and the bit with the light on swished across the copying tray. *Pfft. Like a boss*. It was actually rather enjoyable; I had totally forgotten about the delicious smell of warm toner.

There were exactly 494 pages that needed to be copied, twice. Presuming that his majesty wanted them collated, and provided I pressed the green button manually for each page, I could probably stretch this out all morning.

Ten minutes in and Lauren appeared beside me. "Did you know that you can just pop it all in this feeder tray here and it will scan each side front and back? As long as you take all the staples out, obviously."

I smiled serenely. "Yes, I do, thank you." And I continued to press the green button scanning each page separately.

"Okay then," said Lauren laughing and shaking her head. She made as if to walk away, back to the table in the centre of the room, which currently sat a further four admin staff entombed within a mountain of paperwork, and sticky notes. There were lots and lots of sticky notes, some even stuck to people's arms and chests. I saw the word 'CRAPs' several times.

"Actually," I said, and Lauren stopped in her tracks. "Do you want a cup of coffee? It's half-past eight and I've just realised I haven't had a hot coffee in... eleven months."

"What?" said Lauren, blinking at me.

"Or tea?"

"Uh... wow, yeah OK. Never had a solicitor make us coffee before."

"Really?"

Slightly shamefaced, I made my way to the floor's

kitchenette. "Coffee, everyone?" I said as I passed the mass of CRAPs papers.

Four faces looked up and said "Yes please" with varying degrees of surprise and delight.

I spent the rest of the morning alternating between making coffee for the admin staff and assiduously copying the papers for Ryan. Fifty pages down, a cappuccino. Another fifty down, another cappuccino.

At about 10:00, I walked past the admin desk for the sixth time that morning.

"Oh I'm ok, I couldn't possibly drink another cup of coffee. I'm starting to get shaky, but thanks," said Lauren, holding her stomach, before I could ask again. Only, I wasn't going to.

"I'm not going to the kitchen. I need to express; my boobs are starting to get quite heavy." I held up my handbag to show them the breast pump.

"Where are you going to do that?" said Lauren getting to her feet.

"Um... The toilets." I looked away from their gazes. "That's where I had to do it yesterday. Clive said—"

"Oh fuck Clive! You can do it there if you like." Lauren pointed to an empty desk partially obscured by a row of filing cabinets next to the window.

"Are you sure?"

"Of course, we're not going to let you do it in the toilets."

"God, no," the others chimed in.

I watched the people in the offices across the road from the Caine Reynolds' building as I milked myself with my little handheld pump, like some sort of official business cow (but in a good way). This is what shirts that button up through the middle were made for. In between the suck and release of the pump, I half-listened to the admin staff discussing the intricacies of the CRAPs.

"No, no, Mark did it last year, he won't do it two years in a row. What about Dom?"

"He's going to be in Mexico next week."

"Really? Lucky bastard. Didn't he just get back from Florida?"

"Yes."

There was a collective sigh.

"Who can we get to do it then?"

"Well what about…"

The sudden hushed tones brought me out of my reverie. I stopped squeezing the pump and looked up. Lauren was standing at the end of the desk, and the rest of the admin staff were all leaning back in their seats gawping in my direction.

"What's this about?" I said, my gaze flicking from Lauren to the rest of the team.

"How much work have you got on at the moment, Jaime?" said Lauren, twisting her fingers into her palms.

"Absolutely nothing whatsoever until Clive gets my forms and training up to date. And that really doesn't look like it's about to happen any time soon. Why?"

"Weeeeellll…" Lauren's voice was silky. "We need a really important job done, and we've got no one to do it. Jenny from the Solihul branch was going to do it but she just pulled out, apparently public speaking isn't her—"

"What is it?" I said cutting her short, I wasn't sure if I liked where this was heading.

"We need someone to host the CRAPs. And we've all decided" – the other admins averted their eyes; I think one of them even coughed – "we'd really love it if you could do it. You don't have to do much." Lauren held out her hand silencing my whimpering objections. "You just need to make a very small speech about the company, and how lovely it is to work here, and how amazing our staff are, especially the fee-earners, and then present the award for Lawyer of the Year."

"Um, no thanks I'll pass," I said without hesitation, squeezing the breast pump again.

"I'll put you down as a maybe then," said Lauren, and she walked back over to her desk and sat down.

I was definitely not going to look at them. No way. But I did manage to keep them in the corner of my peripherals, that way it at least *looked* as though I was ignoring them. They were having a whispered and animated conversation, clearly about me and my refusal to host the CRAPs. It wasn't going to work, whatever strategy they were concocting. I really didn't care about the public speaking part, that's not something that has ever bothered me, but it was just the CRAPs themselves. They were always just a bit...well, crap. Every year it was exactly the same thing – cheap booze, crappy venue, and peanuts to eat. Literally peanuts, like the things that cartoon elephants eat, and that was it, no proper food. Not to mention that every year the award nominees were often the same people, most of whom I'd never met.

They were still talking about me. It was an uncomfortable feeling, knowing that I was the current discussion topic, but not actually being able to hear their words, so I resumed staring at the two women in the office across the road. Was it a marketing company? I couldn't remember. The walls were offensively bright and there were incongruous 'creative' spaces, like a ping-pong table, a grand piano, and a collection of pointless beanbags. The two women, who wore suits like mine, were hanging out of an open window smoking cigarettes. They were talking spiritedly, but their voices were lost over the din of cars passing, traffic lights bleeping and the puffy, sucky noise of the breast pump.

"Who's nominated?" I said suddenly. "For Lawyer of the Year. Who's up for nomination?"

"Uh…" Lauren scrambled through bits of paper on the desk, and was handed a handwritten note. She read the names aloud. "Mike Hilton from Gloucester, Meera Shree from Stoke, Claire Taylor from Leamington, Fred McKenna also from Leamington, Ryan Burgess from Birmingham—"

"Urgh!"

"—and Niamh Goode also from Birmingham."

"Oh my god, really!?"

Forgetting that one of my boobs was hanging out and attached to a see-through cone, I jumped out of my seat, ran up to the table, and looked at the piece of paper in Lauren's hand. I wanted to see Niamh's name in writing with my own eyes. Most of the other nominees I knew only from name, or from their intranet photos, but I know that Niamh deserved this recognition, more than anyone on that list and especially more than Ryan. Imagine presenting my best friend with the Lawyer of the Year award.

"So you'll do it then?" Lauren asked, looking everywhere except at my semi-exposed breast.

"Hmm."

In my head the award looked exactly like a BAFTA, despite the betraying memory that it was more like a rubbish glass paperweight or something. I could just picture Niamh's face. But what if she didn't win? Urgh, what if he won? No way could I hand over that beautiful golden mask to him. The thought made my stomach churn. I could always just say Niamh's name, even if she doesn't win – what would they do about that? Would they sack me? Or could I pass it off as an innocent mistake? Baby brain. How would they even know that I fudged the results? Unless... the partners already know who the winner is, and the whole event was just a sham. It usually followed suit that the winner of the award would go on to be promoted, occasionally to partner, and Niamh was very clear about not wanting to become partner. And anyway, what would I even say in my speech? It would be impossible to big up a company that you despised. It's such a backwards place here. Maybe I could say something progressive, inspire some change in my colleagues. Fuck knows some of them need it. Since all the partners from the other branches would be there, it *would* be an excellent opportunity to grab their attention. If my speech was momentous enough, I could show them what great partner material I'm made of, and what fantastic leadership skills I have. They would *have* to consider me for Frances' position. Have to. Frances said that not all the partners think the same way as Clive. But it would need to be a really, really, fucking excellent speech.

I turned away from the table and pulled my boob free of the suction cup, wiped the residual milk off myself and the cup with a wet wipe, and poured the milk into a little pre-labelled bag. I pushed my boob back into my bra, clipped both sides of the bra shut and did the buttons of my shirt back up.

"Okay, yeah, I'll do it," I said, hoping that they considered my pause dramatic.

Lauren bounced to her feet and gave me an awkward one-armed hug, while the rest of the team gave a round of applause. I was already getting the star treatment. I could get used to this.

"I knew we could count on you," one of them said.

"Yes, Jaime, you'll be perfect. Well done," said another.

"Right, I'd better go and put this in the fridge, and then I suppose I should work on my speech – after I finish this photocopying."

I would definitely need a new dress too. Maybe Niamh would come shopping with me on Friday.

That night, I laid my head on the pillow and tucked my phone underneath it. Oliver was already snoring loudly, but I did not hear it for long. Hours later, or perhaps minutes, I was wrenched upwards; I had been dreaming. There was cake involved, and now there was no cake. Instead, my brain and ears were being blasted by an air raid siren…?

I sat bolt upright in bed. The fuzz in my mind cleared after a few seconds. The siren was River – she was crying. I grabbed my phone: 11:45 p.m. I had been asleep for only 45 minutes. Yawning, I stood up and made my way to River's room, knocking into walls and door jambs on the way. The warm happiness of the cake dream faded into the night.

River became silent the moment my boob hit her mouth. I could practically hear that nosey bitch, Carol, from the library; "Ooh you shouldn't be feeding her in the night, she ought to be able to self soothe by now, cry it out, it's the only way she'll learn."

I was still holding my phone in my hand – it's a rookie mistake to leave your phone in another room during night feed duty, and I was no rookie.

"Well done me," I whispered as I unlocked my screen.

There was a DM.

. . .

Hi hun, it's Marie from the ForumFriends group, can you please add me back to the group? I had to delete my account and now I can't find it anymore. I have something I need to tell everyone.

- *Marie Sparks*

Hmm, weird to be messaging this late. I typed back.

Yes of course, you wouldn't be able to find it as the privacy is set to secret. U ok?

- *Jaime Wright*

I am now. I'll explain on the group.

- *Marie Sparks*

I re-added my friend and waited for her message to appear.
Bing.

Marie Sparks - 3rd March - 23:56
 TW.
 This is a hard post to write, but I have to say it. Rob beat me up again last night and I finally left him. I'm in a women's refuge shelter.

I had to delete my ForumFriends account and make a new one. I'll put a picture in the comments. I'm OK now.

I read through Marie's message a second time just to make sure I had understood it properly. River was still suckling quietly, her eyes closed. I held my breath and then scrolled down to see the photo Marie had added. It was Marie's face, but barely recognisable. Her left eye was swollen almost completely closed and it was the colour of midnight sky. The only part of the eyeball that was visible was bright red. Above her eye, there was a two centimetre long gash, a number of sticky, paper stitches cross-hatching it. It had begun to scab. There was a small cut on her lip, like a scabbed cold sore, and a bruise on the left side of her head running the entire breadth of her jawbone.

I couldn't stop looking at it. My pulse quickened, and my throat was closing over. My face was wet too. Silent tear drops splashed onto River's Grobag. It was near impossible to keep my breathing steady; I would wake her up for sure.

The comments from the other moms began appearing faster than I could think.

Natalie Dixon - 3rd March - 23:58
OMG! What a monster! I'm so glad you're safe now. Where is Daisy? Is she harmed?

Carys Honeyman - 3rd March - 23:58
Shit hun! I can't believe he did this again. Where are you now? How are you feeling?

. . .

Ruchi Kapoor - 3rd March - 23:59

Did you call the police? What happens now? Please tell me you're going to press charges this time?

Erin Schellenger - 3rd March - 23:59

I'm so sorry this happened again, you don't deserve any of this. I hope you're safe. Is Daisy with you?

Marie Sparks - 4th March - 00:03

Daisy was hurt, but it was an accident. She got in the way, he didn't mean to hurt her, but she's ok now. I've left him, for good this time. I'm in a women's refuge place in Lincoln. We have our own bedroom, but I'm sharing a living space with two other women and their babies. One of them is only eight weeks old — he's so cute. I called the police, but Rob has done a runner. Probably to his brother's. There's a warrant out for his arrest, but TBH I don't think the police are too bothered about finding him. They said they would put a thing in the wanted section, and that I was safe as long as I'm here. They said I need to put in an application for an injunction, it's like a restraining order, but there's no way it would stop him from trying to contact me. I don't think there's much I can do except wait for the police to arrest him.

I wiped the tears from my face with the sleeve of my pyjamas and began to type with my thumb.

Jaime Wright - 4th March - 00:05

Hun, I'm sure there's something we can do in the meantime. My best friend is a family lawyer, she deals with this sort of case all the time. I will get her to call you tomorrow if that's OK? Sending love. xx

The sickening, constricting feeling in my chest eased a little. It was the least I could do to help, and I wasn't even going to do anything, I was just going to let Niamh handle it. I really hated feeling so useless all the time. Maybe Niamh was right about me and Family law. Still, there was no one better I could think of to help my friend in need.

Buzz.

It was a link to an article in the Lincolnshire Gazette.

Erin Schellenger - 4th March - 00:07
Just seen this.

A Lincolnshire man is wanted by police after he allegedly assaulted his wife in the early hours of this morning.

Police were called to the couple's home at around 3 a.m. on the morning of 3rd March after neighbours heard shouts. The man's wife and nine-month old baby were later taken to hospital.

Robert Sparks, 38, a plumber from the Gainsborough area, is said to have fled the scene before the officers arrived. He is believed to be driving a black Audi TT and may be in the Lincolnshire area or the Midlands. He is well known to Lincoln Police. The force are now appealing to anyone who may have information on his whereabouts to come forward.

There was a non-emergency contact number, an email address, and a link to the Crime Stoppers page.

And a picture of Rob's face. It was a mugshot style photo, I guess from a previous arrest. He was smiling. It was a small crooked smirk that was barely visible on his lips, yet apparent in his eyes. An 'inside-joke' kind of smile. I felt the swooping sick feeling in my throat again. Obviously, this picture was taken before he beat up Marie, but I couldn't help the feeling that he was laughing at her, or what he had just done.

He was a rather unremarkable looking man. His hair was closely cropped, either dark brown or black, he had small dark eyes which crinkled at the corners, a slightly too-short nose, and a tattoo on the left side of his neck. I squinted at the photo in the dark to better make out the design. It looked, though I couldn't be completely sure, like a bulldog, wearing a top hat and smoking a cigar.

WTAF.

River was now fast asleep. I lowered her into her cot, and then sat right back down in the breastfeeding chair, illuminated by the phone's blue glow once again. The other moms and I stayed up another hour or so, consoling our friend ("you're safe now, you've done the right thing by calling the police"), lambasting her husband ("what an evil man, who could hurt someone they love?"), and assuaging our own observer's guilt ("I'm sure they'll catch him soon. Let us know if we can help"). After a while, it appeared that Marie had gone to sleep, as she stopped responding to messages. I traipsed back to my own bed, and climbed under the covers, the feeling of uselessness clawing at my pyjama collar. Hours I lay there, checking my phone for notifications every ten minutes or so. Eventually I drifted off into an uneasy sleep filled with crying babies, BAFTA awards, and shit tattoos.

The final message that went unanswered was this:

. . .

Kelly Vaughan – 4th March – 02:18
  Just out of interest where does Rob's brother live?

The next morning, I sat at Ryan's desk and attempted to write a forward-thinking, feminist speech of such earth-shattering importance that the partners would have to sit up and take notice of me. The events of last night had given me the impetus to make a real go at the position in Family. I needed to be helping people. And that was that. I tried to imagine what Marie must be going through; in an unfamiliar place, with unfamiliar people, a nine-month old baby, and a busted face, and I just couldn't. I couldn't even *imagine* it. The only thing I could be sure of was the way I felt about a man I had only ever read about online. It was forcing me to rethink my life and make myself a better person. Anger can be a great tool to drive change. Sure, the position in Family would be hard, and I was definitely going to have to learn to be tougher, make actual plans, and see them through – thanks Niamh – but the satisfaction that would come from knowing I was making a difference in the world, surely far outweighed any negatives. I needed this job now, and that was why this speech had to be phenomenal.

~~Hello~~
  ~~Welcome~~
  ~~Hello~~
  Hi everybody

Words hate me.

I rocked side to side on the chair, hoping that inspiration would magically strike. A solid two minutes of swaying about had, however, begun to take its toll. My head was spinning, the room was moving, and vomit loitered at the back of my throat. I threw my head back on the chair and pressed my fingers to my eyelids.

"Urrrggggggghhhh."

"A little birdie told me you're going to present the CRAPs this year?" An Irish-Brummie voice squeaked closer.

I took my fingers away from my eyes, the room was still spinning. It was like being back at uni.

"Ooh, is this your speech?"

I swept the sheet of A4 into Ryan's desk drawer, but too late. Niamh snatched the piece of paper as it fell.

Through gasping breaths of laughter, she said, "Well, it's a start."

"Urgh it's so hard!" I said, throwing my head back again, and pushing myself away from the desk. "It has to be really good and I can't think of anything to say."

"I know why you're doing it; I think it's a good idea. All the partners together at once. You'll need Frances to put forward a recommendation for you though."

"Oh right, OK."

"If you're genuinely interested, I'll talk to her today."

"Bostin. Thanks."

"No problem. At least you'd be on my side of the floor, that's something."

I smiled and then I remembered Marie. "Oh, actually, there is something you can help me with, it's not about the job though."

I explained to Niamh all about Marie and the safe house and Rob, and that I'd told Marie that Niamh would call her today.

"Of course I will, poor woman. How awful for her. Have you got her number? I'll give her a call before lunch and talk her through her options."

I wheeled forward on my seat, crouched under Ryan's desk, and began to rummage through my handbag for my phone.

"Jaime, there is something I need to tell you." Niamh sounded distant and wary, but because there was a whole desktop between us I couldn't see her expression. "On Friday I've got an interv—"

"Sorry to interrupt," said a voice that was neither Niamh's nor Ryan's. I smacked the back of my head into the underside of the desk.

Ouch.

Rachel was standing next to Niamh, her arms clasped in front of her. "Jaime, I've got Paul from the building's main desk on the phone, he said that there's a client of yours in the lobby."

"A client of mine?" I said, rubbing my head. "I don't have any clients yet. Unless it's an old one? Why are they downstairs?" I glanced at Niamh, who looked equally as perplexed and intrigued.

The three of us walked to the reception desk.

"Did you get a name?" I asked.

"Hmm, I think he said his name was Mr. Smith," said Rachel with a shrug.

I've probably had a thousand clients named Mr. Smith.

Behind the reception counter there was a large display screen that split into four parts, each showing a different view from CCTV cameras around the building and offices. Rachel pressed the image in the top right corner, and it became full screen. It showed the main reception desk and lobby area, so stark white it looked like the room had been bleached. In the foreground stood the suited figure of Paul, the doorman. He was holding the phone receiver to his head and facing away from the camera. In the middle of the image stood the figure of another man, more casually dressed in jeans, a white T shirt and an open, grey hoodie. This was obviously Mr. Smith, but I didn't recognise him.

I leaned in closer. "I don't know who that is. I don't think that's an old client." I squinted, as though squinting would change the focus of the security camera.

The man was standing still, his hands rooted in his pockets. He casually looked from Paul to the door, back to Paul, and then at the camera. Directly at the camera.

I gasped and jumped backwards.

"Holy fuck! That's him! That's Rob! Marie's husband!"

CHAPTER THREE

"Oh my god what?! How do you know?" said Niamh.

"I know it's him." I clutched at my shirt buttons; it was getting quite hot in reception. "Look at his stupid tattoo."

"It looks like a dog wearing a hat?" said Rachel, her eyebrows raised towards me.

"Fuck! What are we going to do?" My mind was blank. I looked from Niamh to Rachel to the monitor.

"Make him wait in the lobby, Rach," said Niamh, taking the lead. "I'm going to call the police. He's a wanted criminal."

I watched the screen. The area beyond it was going dark.

Rachel picked up the receiver and said in an upbeat tone. "Hi Paul, it turns out he's a wanted criminal. Can you get him to wait in the lobby while we call the police? Thank you."

Niamh took her phone out of her jacket pocket. I was

only vaguely aware of what she was saying. "Hello, yes police please…"

On the screen Paul hung up the receiver, and with an infinitesimal glance towards the camera, he indicated to a row of waiting chairs near the panelled windows. Rob turned his head in the direction of the chairs and walked a few steps. He paused. For a few seconds he stood stock-still in the centre of the screen, he was staring at Paul. The clarity of the picture made it impossible to read his facial expression, but his left foot was pointing towards the glass door. Paul must have clocked it too because he maneuvered himself in front of the reception desk, just as Rob took one final, fleeting look at the camera and ran straight out of the door. Paul reached the door a fraction of a second after Rob, but it was too late. He whirled on the spot just outside, hovered for a few moments, and returned to the desk.

My heart was pummelling the inside of my chest.

Paul picked the receiver back up. Rachel was still holding hers limply at her side, she lifted it back to her ear. I could see Paul's mouth moving.

"What did he do?" Rachel asked me. "Why's he a wanted criminal?"

"He beat up his wife and put her in hospital," I said without looking away from the screen. Though this seemed to be getting dark too.

Rachel relayed this to Paul. On the screen he shook his head.

"Okay, thank you," said Niamh, sliding back into focus. Rachel and I looked at her; the room span dangerously around me. "They said they might send someone out. They didn't say when though. They'll probably want to take a statement from all of us. And they'll probably want a copy of that." She pointed at the screen.

Rachel nodded, immediately sat down and pulled the keyboard towards herself.

I got the feeling Niamh was being overly optimistic about how involved the police would get in this situation.

"How does he know who you are? And where you work? And why was he here?" said Niamh. Her face was pale.

"I have no idea," I mumbled. "I really need to sit down actually. I feel lightheaded."

Rachel jumped out of her seat, and I crumpled into a heap, tit-planting the chair. My knees smashed against the carpet.

"No, you need to lie on the floor like this." Rachel pushed me, by the forehead, into a lying position on the ground. "And put your feet up on my chair like this. I did a first aid course – this is what you're supposed to do."

She grabbed my legs and heaved them up onto the seat, my skirt fell to my pelvis, revealing my black M&S mega-pants. Rachel then pulled a rusty old fan out from underneath the desk and aimed it downwards towards my face, my hair whipping all around as it swung from side to side.

It was at this exact moment Clive entered reception.

"Morning Rache—" He must have caught sight of me lying on the floor with my knickers on show and my hair wrapped around my face. He laughed, a cruel, dismissive bark. "Gunning for a promotion aye Jaime?"

"She's just had a very traumatic experience, actually," said Rachel, attempting, and failing, to keep the hair from my face. "A wanted criminal just came to see her."

A wanted criminal just came to see me.

I pushed myself up into a sitting position.

"Right, whatever," whispered Clive. "Oh Jaime, I

haven't had a chance to put through your paperwork yet, just in case you were going to ask." He walked off.

I wasn't. But maybe I was overreacting about Rob. Just because he's a wanted criminal doesn't *necessarily* mean he meant me any harm, right? Perhaps I should have given him the benefit of the doubt. Maybe he just wanted to talk. But why? Why was here? How did he know me and where I worked? Why was he involving me, of all the moms on the group?

Argh. My head was going to explode.

"I think I need to message Marie and the other moms," I said. I got to my feet, still shaking, and smoothed out my skirt and hair.

"You can use the boardroom if you like, Jaime," said Rachel. "No one has booked it until eleven today."

I clutched the edge of the boardroom table so tightly that my knuckles turned white. I took only a few moments to compose myself and then began to type out a message on the moms' group.

Jaime Wright - 4th March - 09:32
Guys, I'm kinda freaked out. Pretty sure Rob just came to my work building. We called the police, but he ran before we had a chance to find out why he was here. I don't know how he knows my name, or where I work, but he asked for me personally. I don't know what to do. Why was he here?

Georgia Kerr - 4th March - 09:34
WTF

. . .

Natalie Dixon - 4th March - 09:36
OMG that's so scary. Are you OK?

Jamie Wright - 4th March - 09:37
*@**Marie Sparks** Just tagging you so that you can see this thread.*

Marie Sparks - 4th March - 09:44
Oh no. Guys, I'm so sorry. I'm so so sorry. I didn't want to say anything in case I frightened you all for nothing, but the reason we fought the other night was because he found out about the group on my ForumFriends app and he saw the threads that I posted before about the last time he beat me. He was especially upset about Jaime's comment saying that I should leave him right away and that I could call her at the solicitors where she worked. He told me that I needed to give him all of your full names and addresses. I said I didn't know your addresses. And then he got really mad and that's when he beat me. I honestly don't think he would harm you. He just says these things when he's angry. It's all my fault.

Jaime Wright - 4th March - 09:46
It's not your fault hun. You had too much on your mind to remember to tell us everything that went on. Just one thing though, how did he know my name and where I worked?

Marie Sparks - 4th March - 09:49
He screenshot the page where it says the list of members. That's why I had to delete my account, but I think he has it on his phone now.

. . .

Erin Schellenger - 4th March - 09:53
  If you Google 'Jaime Wright' the first thing you get is your work profile.

Erin had included a link. My online work bio, featuring a photo that was taken when I first joined the practice eight years ago. My hair was shorter and trendier, my face was thinner and yet more full, and I wore an optimistic and eager smile. There's a good chance he wouldn't recognise me from this photo. Though, if he'd gone onto my Forum-Friends page he'd have seen a photo of me holding River, that one was only taken at Christmas.

Molly Cheung - 4th March - 10:03
  Will he come back?

Jaime Wright - 4th March - 10:04
  The doorman has printed off his picture and put it on the building's staff board so that if he does come back they will citizen's arrest him right there and then.

Marie Sparks - 4th March - 10:06
  I really doubt he would come back. He's not stupid.

Erin Schellenger - 4th March - 10:06
  Who else's information does he have?

There was a long wait. Those three little dots kept flashing up with the text 'Marie is typing' and then disappearing.

Marie Sparks - 4th March - 10:09
I'm not sure. I guess everyone's if he can Google you. He doesn't have access to the group anymore.

Ruchi Kapoor - 4th March - 10:10
But he has a screenshot of everyone's names?

Dot dot dot... Dot dot dot...

Marie Sparks - 4th March - 10:12
Yes.

Marie Sparks - 4th March - 10:13
He's mostly just pissed off with Jaime though because she is admin of the group and because of the things she said about me leaving him. He blames her for what happened on Sunday night. I don't think that he'd try and make contact again though.

"Fuck!"

Niamh who had been patiently sitting beside me in the boardroom jumped out of her chair.

"What is it?"

"I think he's out to get me. He blames *me*! Marie is trying to protect him I think, or herself, I'm not sure. She says that he won't come and look for me anymore, but…" I shrugged.

"What does your gut tell you?"

I rubbed my forehead. It all just felt so weird, like something was not adding up. I'm usually such a great judge of character, but it is impossible to know if you are being lied to over a computer. I felt like my questions haven't been properly answered. If she held back information like this last night, would she hold anything else back? What is this man – who put his own wife in hospital – capable of doing to me?

"I think he wants revenge," I said, and then because that sounded stupid out loud, I added, "or something. He thinks it's all my fault that he beat her up the other night and that he's now on the run. I kept telling her to leave him, to get out, take the baby and go, and that if she needed help, I knew an amazing family solicitor that could. I kept saying it to her. We all did really, but I was really persistent. He found those messages and now he's really fucking angry."

"What do you think he wants to do?"

I shook my head. "I don't know. Would he have beaten me up if he got the chance today or maybe just yelled at me?"

Niamh stared blankly at me. She did not have the answer to that question. "Well you need to tell the police this when they come. You probably shouldn't stay at yours tonight in case he knows your address. Do you have anywhere you could go tonight? Your dad's? Or Colleen's? You can stay at ours if you like. But…oh… Ingrid's just getting over chicken pox, and you'd have to all share one room. Mike and I can go in William's room and you can take ours. I'd doubt he'd come back here though – you'll be safe here, at work. If he does come back, he'll be arrested instantly. Do you think he knows that? Maybe we could lure him back and then—"

"Wait." I held out my hand and Niamh fell silent. Lightbulb! "That's it. We could lure him back here... or somewhere and then call the police. Great idea Niamh!"

"Wait, wait, no, that's a terrible idea," she said shaking her hands at me. "Just let the police deal with him."

I ignored her. "Judging by the way he was on camera I don't think he'd come back here, but maybe... if we could find out a bit more..." I broke off mid-thought.

Her eyes were wide and she shook her head from side to side, but I was already running through ways that we could catch him. The police didn't seem particularly bothered about finding him, but maybe if we could track down his friends, or his brother... Anyway, it would be better than sitting around and waiting for him to punch my lights out.

I felt a surge of adrenaline, or possibly hunger, and began tapping away fiercely on my phone.

Jaime Wright - 4th March - 10:18
OK I've just been thinking, and I've come to the conclusion that we need to stop him. I don't feel comfortable knowing that he's out there with all our details and that he might come at any time to any of our works or homes. I think we need to find out where he is, or trick him to go somewhere, and then call the police on him.

Kelly Vaughan - 4th March - 10:23
Ooh, a vigilante mission. I love it!

Marie Sparks - 4th March - 10:24
Really? How are we going to do that?

. . .

Jaime Wright - 4th March - 10:24

No, you stay put hun, you're safe where you are. Let me have a think. Maybe I could convince him to hand himself in. Do you know how we might find him? What's his brother's address?

Marie Sparks - 4th March - 10:25

No sorry. He lives in Birmingham. It's something like Whitecross, or Whitechapel, or White-something Road. I told the police this, but they didn't seem interested. They just told me to let them know if I remember the full address. But they must have Brad's address, he's always getting arrested. I just think they don't really care.

Jaime Wright - 4th March - 10:27

OK. I'll think of something and let you all know my plan. I might need some help though.

Erin Schellenger - 4th March - 10:28

Let me know what I can do. I'm in the Cotswolds, so not too far from you.

Kelly Vaughan - 4th March - 10:29

Happy to help nail that bastard.

I put the phone down on the table and leaned back in the chair. I smiled at Niamh. "We're going on a vigilante mission."

"You seem very happy about this," said Niamh, her mouth pulled down at the sides.

"It's a bit more exciting that photocopying huh?"

"Jaime if I were you, I would just tell the police and let them deal with it, and you focus on writing your speech for the CRAPs."

"Yes, both things *are* important," I said, trying to keep the sarcasm from my voice. "I can write my speech in the daytime at work, and then by night, I can pursue justice." I pretended to flip my hair over my shoulder.

"And who's going to look after River?"

"Oh, so I can't be a vigilante criminal hunter *and* a mother at the same time?" I rolled my eyes, but I could not stop myself from smiling. Finally, I could do something useful.

"Hun, I just want you to be safe. And River too. This is a man that put your friend in hospital. You don't know what he's capable of. I mean, if this is something he does to somebody he apparently loves... what do you think he could do to you? And you're just going to willingly walk right up to him and… What? What are you going to do?"

I hadn't thought that far ahead yet – damn it, Niamh was right about me and my plans – but I would come up with something, I couldn't just do nothing.

"If I sit back and wait for the police to pull their fingers out who knows how long that could be. I'd be more at risk if I do nothing, he could come back at any time. Not to mention all the other moms too. They might not all be able to camp out at their mother-in-law's until then." I shook my head. There was no way in hell I would stay at Colleen's. No thanks. I'd rather have a faceoff with Rob. "I have to do something, Niamh. I have to."

She bit her lip and squinted her eyes at me. This was her 'I can't stop you, can I?' face.

"I promise that I won't put myself in any unnecessary

danger. I'll make sure that there's a big group of us... for safety. I've already got volunteers."

Niamh said nothing. Her mouth was pulled into a wide grimace. I thought maybe she was going to be sick. I took this to mean: "OK Jaime, you do what you need to."

Later I went back to the admin office to express milk again. It was such a relaxing atmosphere in there, with the window open and the spring breeze pouring in and the non-horrible colleagues. I began to think about my speech for the CRAPs; at least if I got that over and done with maybe Niamh would lay off me about the criminal-hunting mission. Maybe I could say something about taking justice into your own hands. Yeah, that would fit in nicely with a speech about a law firm. OK, Caine Reynolds was mostly a private client firm, and there wasn't much in the way of reclaiming justice. I haven't even set foot in a courtroom since I became fully qualified. But all that could change. Family was the one real area of this firm where you had proper 'cases'.

I found, however, that I couldn't concentrate on speech writing at all. Instead, my mind kept wandering off to implausible scenarios in which I kick down the door to Rob's brother's house and one-punch Rob in the chest. He flies backwards through the air, and with Jackie Chan reflexes I catch him by the wrist, spin him around and slap handcuffs on him. Then I will say something really cool like... Well, hopefully I'll think of something cool to say before that moment.

"What are you so happy about?" sniped Ryan, as I walked back into the Chamber.

"Nothing." I sat down on the chair next to him and

chucked my bag on the floor.

"We've got a client meeting at eleven," he said.

"Oh, excellent," I said, jumping back to my feet. It was 10:55.

"Woah, wait. No. I should've said *I* have a client meeting. I need *you* to make the drinks." He sat back in his chair, folded his arms and gave me a smirk, which gave me a nearly unquashable urge to punch him in the mouth.

"No. First photocopying and now drinks. That's not my job! I'm an associate."

"An associate that brings coffee."

Ryan got to his feet too. He towered at least a foot over me blocking out the light from the fluorescent bulbs, and glared down, his eyes narrowed, and his disgusting smile still did not falter. Perhaps he was challenging me. When I didn't say anything he added, "And bring some of those individually wrapped biscuits too, the daughter is really fit." He turned and began walking away.

"Urgh, what a prick," I murmured under my breath.

"What did you say?" he said, stopping abruptly two desks away.

"I said," I began, as loud as I could through gritted teeth, "what should I pick? Should I pick the plain biscuits? Or. Should. I. Pick. The. Almond. Ones?"

Ryan's smile dropped, and then he began speaking as though I were a toddler incapable of following simple instructions. "Just bring three lattes into the board room in ten minutes."

FML. I shouldn't be making coffees, I had far more important things to plan, like wreaking justice, also my feminist agenda.

Ten minutes later I stomped over to the kitchenette. It was as simple as putting a cup under a spout and pressing a button, but it was not what I'd spent years training to do. I threw the biscuits on the tray with such incredible force that all but two flew right off the other end and onto the floor.

"Fuck. My. Life," I muttered, as I bent down to pick up the stupid things.

"Thank you so much, Jaime," said Ryan in his saccharine 'client' voice.

"You're welcome," I said trying to match the affected nauseating tone. I placed the tray bearing the coffees and over-packaged biscuits on the boardroom table in front of Ryan, but before I removed my hands I turned to him, my hair falling in front of my face so that the two clients sitting opposite couldn't see, and gave him an expression that I really hoped he would read as 'maybe I spat in your coffee'.

"Will your assistant be joining us?" said the older of the two women. She must have been in her 70s; she wore well-looked-after clothes and had perfectly coiffed, shiny copper hair. She spoke with a deep, earthy voice.

Ryan laughed and opened his mouth to speak.

I sidestepped in front of him. "I'm not his assistant. I'm an associate solicitor. Actually, I make much more money that he does." I gave him a satisfyingly petulant smile.

"But—" began Ryan.

The woman cut him off. "Bloody good for you!" She banged her hand down on the table, making the cups and cutlery rattle. She looked at Ryan. "You're the one that ought to be making the coffees then, eh?" she said with a deep laugh.

Ryan flushed bright red and began fumbling with his papers on the table.

"Say you will join us," said the woman. "It'd be nice to

have a woman's sensitivity here; I have just lost my husband after all." She didn't look the least bit sad about it.

A sordid, insensitive thought flashed through my mind, one that often happens when I'm watching crime dramas: *you did it*. I shook it away. I should have made my excuses right there and then and left Ryan to his own clients, but something made me hesitate. It was probably that hideous sycophantic smile he'd given me earlier. I wanted to rub salt into his wound. I liked this woman. I liked her deep, ballsy voice and her no-nonsense attitude, and I wanted to see Ryan suffer at her hands. Maybe I could even pick up some tips from her.

Instead of leaving, like Ryan was clearly trying to indicate with his rapid eyebrow movements that I should, I found my arm stretching out to take her hand.

"I'm Bea Montgomery." She leaned forward and we shook hands.

"Jaime Wright."

The younger of the two women leaned forward. "Kate. Bea's daughter."

"Nice to meet you." I sat in the chair next to Ryan and pulled it up to the table. If I looked directly at him, I might have burst out laughing. I was probably going to get into trouble for this, but it was so worth it, just to get one over on that buffoon.

"Absolutely great meeting you, Jaime. I feel so much better knowing you'll be handling everything from here. Nice to meet you too, Ryan." Bea shook my hand and then Ryan's.

We were standing outside the boardroom, in front of reception. Rachel was gawping over the top of her monitor at us.

"Thanks for all your help," said Kate, looking only at me.

Ryan and I watched the two women walk back through the foyer area and get in the lift, our 'client' smiles fixed firmly in place.

"Never do that again," Ryan spat once the doors to the lift pinged closed. His eyes flashed, and he began stomping off into the Chamber. I followed in his wake. "You made me look proper yampy. In front of my clients! Do you even know who they are?"

Ooh, he must be pissed; his accent was showing. We have our posh client voices which we could present the BBC news with – Niamh calls them our telephone voices – and then we have our drunken/hanging out with our family/angry AF voices, and that's when the true Brummie appears.

"I'm sorry, Ryan, but you did seem to struggle a bit in that meeting. I never meant to step on your toes... It's just that..." I chose my words carefully. "I have a lot more experience in will writing, and client meetings in general, and you seemed to be... floundering...a bit."

Why was I even apologising? I had done nothing wrong. I didn't think.

"I would've been fine if you hadn't gate-crashed."

"They asked me to stay."

"You should have said no. I got flustered. I was outnumbered." Ryan threw his files onto the desk.

I really wanted to tell him to grow up and stop whining. That he was only mad at me because I'm better at my job than he is at his. That he shouldn't be perving on clients, that he's a sad, disgusting creep. And that having excessively packaged biscuits is unacceptable in a time where everyone is trying to reduce their plastic waste. Fuck the turtles – my client is too attractive, right?

What I actually said: "I'm sorry. It won't happen again. OK?"

It's just what we've been conditioned to do as women: apologise for making a man feel inferior.

What century even is this?

Ryan blew air from his nostrils like an angry, cartoon bull, and acknowledged my apology only by closing his eyes, as if to regain his composure. Like he was the bigger person. Fuck him. He sat down on his chair, placed his hand on the stack of meeting files and, without looking, slid them towards me.

"Type this up will you?" he said.

"Not right now," I muttered, through the smallest gap in my lips. "I've got to pick my daughter up from nursery."

River had Forest School that afternoon. That child had a more exciting schedule than I did. At least the rain had stopped from yesterday. I sat on a sawn-off tree stump and watched my beautiful offspring grow muddier and muddier. Eventually I gave up trying to wipe the mud off at around the same time River decided she wanted to eat leaves instead of the lovingly quartered grapes I had packed. Whatever. I heard that a little bit of mud is good for you anyway, helps you build a healthy immune system. At least that's what I'll say when the other moms start whispering about me and shaking their heads again.

I needn't have worried though; the other moms seemed to be doing just as shit a job at keeping their babies clean as I was. And there was always that one mum, Abbey I think her name was, who's equally as muddy as her child – worse even.

The best part about Forest School was that it provided

ample thinking time, so by the time I was stripping River down and putting her in the car seat I had the beginnings of a plan to secure the capture of Rob Sparks. Largely inspired by my new friend, Bea (I'm still convinced her husband didn't *fall* down the stairs), and my new desire to prove Niamh wrong about my disastrous planning abilities.

Once River was in bed that night, and I'd started on tea, I would ask the other moms for their help.

Jaime Wright - 4th March - 19:18

Right mommies, who's good at social media stalking? I've been thinking of ways that we can make Rob hand himself in. But first, we need to find him.

Erin Schellenger - 4th March - 19:23

I am. I run a vlog and I'm reeeeeeaaaallly good at mining social media. What do you want me to find out about him?

Jaime Wright - 4th March - 19:24

I need to know his plans. Is he working? Does he have any parties or events planned? And if so what are they? My plan is to corner him somewhere, and preferably somewhere in public, because if he's going to get violent, he will be less likely to do it if there are a lot of other people around.

Erin Schellenger - 4th March - 19:26

OK, give me a couple of hours. I'll see what I can get on him.

Marie Sparks - 4th March - 19:26

Just a heads-up, Rob doesn't have a ForumFriends profile so you might find it difficult to track him down. You might try looking up his brother, Bradley Sparks, but I don't know what his privacy settings are like. He would never 'friend' me, and I deleted my account anyway.

Erin Schellenger - 4th March - 19:27
No problem, I love a good challenge.

I plugged my phone into the charge point by the cooker and began to collect ingredients and apparatus from the kitchen. I was in the middle of chopping an onion – a spoon held in between my teeth because I had heard to do that to stop yourself from crying – when my phone buzzed on the counter.

Anyway, who doesn't have a ForumFriends profile in this day and age? Weirdo.

Erin Schellenger - 4th March - 19:48
I've found him. Turns out Bradley's privacy settings are absolute wank. It looks like they'll both be going to Wolverhampton Racecourse next Friday for the Royal Spring Charity Cup. You might have to wear your posh things. Is that OK? Or do you want me to keep looking?

Ruchi Kapoor - 4th March - 19:49
Can't you just tell the police that Rob will be at the races and let them take care of it?

Erin Schellenger - 4th March - 19:50

I've already rung them. Anonymously of course. They said that this information is too speculative for them to act on, and to contact them again if we have anything more concrete. Sorry, I tried. Looks like Jaime's right, we'll have to do this on our own. If we can just go to the races and make sure he's there we can call them then.

Yeah after we have a chat with him.

Jaime Wright - 4th March - 19:50
Next Friday? I have my work's presentation thing in the evening.

Erin Schellenger - 4th March - 19:51
So, the races finish at 3 p.m. If your work's thing isn't until the evening, I think you'd have enough time to get back for it. Shall I meet you at the racecourse?

Jaime Wright - 4th March - 19:52
Yes please. That would be great.

Carys Honeyman - 4th March - 19:56
I can be there too. The more of us that go the safer we'll be, right?

Kelly Vaughan - 4th March - 19:57
Like I said before, can't wait to nail that prick. Meet at midday?

"You're not on that bloody phone again?" said Oliver,

appearing in the kitchen. He was carrying a white plastic bag that clinked as he walked. It was a sound that brought illicit joy to my heart. "I've been outdoor."

I spat the spoon onto the counter with a flick of my head.

"Guess what?" I didn't wait for him to guess. "I'm on a vigilante mission."

I explained to him all about the unexpected arrival of Rob Sparks at Caine Reynolds, and how I initially freaked the fuck out, but now I had it all under control and he was going down.

"Down, down, down, Rob Sparks is going down," I sang.

"Absolute lunatic," Oliver said. "Do you want me to beat him up?"

"No, Olly," I said holding up my hand. "Let me handle it. I've got a plan." I smiled, I scooped up the chopped onion and threw it into the frying pan.

"Going full Mamabear? As long as you don't try to talk the bastard around!"

Buzz.

Erin Schellenger - 4th March - 20:05

*There's something else I found out. I'm not sure if you know this @**Marie** I'm sorry if you're finding out for the first time now. But Rob has a girlfriend.*

Jaime Wright - 4th March - 20:06
WTF

Molly Cheung - 4th March - 20:07

OMG really?

Marie Sparks - 4th March - 20:09
Fuck 😣

Marie Sparks - 4th March - 20:09
I have suspected for a while.

Erin Schellenger - 4th March - 20:10
Wait, sorry, there's more.

Erin shared a photo to the thread. The picture had been posted by a woman named Ella Ritchie – she must be the other woman – and it was captioned 'So this just happened'. The photo showed Rob and a blonde-haired woman sitting on a red leather sofa in someone's living room, which appeared not to have been decorated since the 90s – it had a border around the middle of the room and the top and bottom of the walls were wallpapered in wildly contrasting, primary-coloured patterns.

Ew.

One of Rob's arms rested around the woman's shoulders, his fingers pressing into her flesh. His other arm clasped her hand, pushing it towards the camera, clearly displaying a silver-coloured diamond ring.

CHAPTER FOUR

"I suppose you'd better take these," said Rachel, the next morning at work.

I had been, up until this point, attempting to write my CRAPs speech, but had so far only succeeded in aligning everything on Ryan's desk into perfect right angles. I had also organised all the pens that I could find in and around Ryan's drawers, first by colour, then by size, until I had a perfect little plastic rainbow. That was, until I foolishly yelled: "Guys if anyone needs any pens, Ryan's got about a million of them here." And thereupon descended chaos. One time, my family and I went on holiday to St. Ives. My sister and I were about nine and ten years old respectively, and this one memory really sticks out in my mind: there was an elderly couple, some Cornish pasties, and, not so much a flock of seagulls but rather an onslaught. That poor old couple never saw it coming. The old woman even had her hand cut open. This incident with Ryan's pens and the rest of the Chamber staff was bringing it all back. They stripped his desk near clean, leaving only a solitary gnawed green biro. That's fine, whatever; I could still write my speech with a green pen. If only I could think of something to write.

Rachel coughed.

"Oh sorry," I said, looking up at her.

"Ryan's called in sick today, so you'd better take them." She handed me a small stack of date-stamped mail, all addressed to Ryan.

"What's wrong with him?" It was difficult to keep the smile from my face.

Rachel was also smiling. "He told Clive he's got food poisoning." She laughed through her nose. "But Clive said that his ego's been bruised, and he needs a few days to recover."

Ooh, a Ryan-free day – imagine all the speech writing I could get done.

"Thanks," I said, thumbing through the small stack of letters. At the bottom was a brown unopened internal mail envelope. Each predecessors' name had been crossed out and the new recipient written underneath, at the very bottom was 'Jamie'.

Spelled my name wrong.

I unwound the once-white-now-yellowy-brown-from-people's-greasy-fingers bit of string that kept the envelope closed and took out the piece of paper within.

Jamie, Ryan's off. Please stand in for him on his client meetings today
 Clive

Yes!

It took me approximately four and a half minutes to get back into my old stride. I smoothed down my suit, pulled my hair back into a – hopefully – neat-ish twist, and necked my fifth espresso of the morning. I was buzzing. Literally and figuratively. Ryan's schedule

meant that I had two client meetings in the morning, and one in the early afternoon. It was

will writing, and they were high profile clients, which meant either rich or famous or both. The latter appointment was with a West Brom footballer, whom surprisingly I had heard of,

and would make Oliver seethingly jealous when I told him that night. I'd had to call River's nursery and see if it was OK to delay her pick-up, and I'd also had to cancel breastfeeding group and baby sign class, but it was OK because both those things are boring AF, and it was worth it to feel constructive again. Like my old self.

I didn't get any speech writing done, but I was so buoyed by the end of the day, I felt confident that something would occur to me before next Friday evening. In fact, even if I hadn't thought of anything to say by then, going off how I felt right now, I could probably just freestyle the whole gig and still get a standing ovation.

One week down, one to go. My first week back to work had come to an end. HR wanted to ease me back in – 'phased return' they called it – so today I had the whole day off. I still dropped River to nursery at 7:30 a.m.

It had been a long time since I'd had a whole morning to myself. No River, no Olly, no responsibilities. I was going to make the most of it.

Deciding that it was probably too early for wine, I poured myself a glass of Kaluha – because it's quite breakfasty – and took it up to the bathroom. While I was running a bath – a bath! – with salts and Molton Brown oils that Olly had bought me for Christmas three years ago but was too special to use and had since been collecting dust under the bed, I had a lovely big, peaceful poo. I could have been holding it in for years. You just can't have a satisfying poo when you're on your own with a baby. But this one, wow, this one more than made up for the nine months of terrible defecation. Longer if you count pregnancy because that really messes with your bowel functions. Another thing people never tell you before you get pregnant. I felt toddler-level pleased, and infallible; everything is much better after a good poo. I even briefly considered posting on the mom's group about it, they would, no doubt, understand my satisfaction.

I lit a candle to mask the... aroma – Midnight Jasmine from Yankee – put Lizzo on Spotify, and climbed into the scalding, perfumed water. It was so hot I had to lower myself in inch by inch, puffing like a steam train.

I didn't realise how tense my muscles had been before, until I could feel how relaxed they became in the water. God this was good, it felt so good. The combination of my magical poo and the power of the bath water made me unbeatable. I could do anything right now. I could probably win the next general election, or Eurovision for Great Britain even, it felt that good.

I sipped my alcoholic, coffee-flavoured, milk, and fleetingly wondered about the calorie content of Kaluha, but even as the thought occurred to me, I dismissed it. I didn't really care. Diets are stupid anyway, just another means to control women. Make us so preoccupied with what we put in our mouths and how we look that we don't have any leftover time or energy to overthrow the patriarchy. *Pfft.*

Our lives are about being controlled. I thought of Rob and Marie, and how he used fear, violence, and years and years of gaslighting to bend her every fibre to his control. Is she still under his will now, still defending him, still lying for him? It definitely feels like there's something she's not telling me. Would she ever get control back? Would she even want it? Then I thought of Clive – why can't he get his bloody ass in gear and get onto HR about my return-to-work forms and training reassessments? Was he doing it on purpose? Keeping me back from practicing my job? But why? Was it about controlling me all along?

I would need to take matters into my own hands. Just like I was doing with Rob. Why was I waiting for a man to do it for me? On Monday morning I was going to march straight into the office and get right on the phone to HR; demand they sort out my training. Why didn't I just do this at the beginning? Why have I been letting everyone walk all over me? Clive, Ryan, even those BMW wankers in Tesco. No, no, no, not anymore. I was taking it all back.

And since I was taking control of my own life and not waiting for men to do stuff for me, I was finally going to put the fucking suitcases back in the loft.

This is what I need to talk about in my speech. All of this (except the suitcases bit) about taking control of our own lives. Fuck diets. Fuck domestic abuse. Fuck the glass ceiling. I'm about to catch a wanted criminal, and then I'm going to get promoted to partner. How's that for taking back control?

I jumped out of the bath with such vigour that I sent a deluge of water in every direction, flooding the bathroom floor. I ran full-pelt down the stairs, naked and streaming with runoff, into the kitchen where the shopping list pad and the shitty fake Sharpie – that was near enough dry –

lay. And I began to write down everything I had thought about in the bath with such speed and ferocity that Usain Bolt would be asking for tips. If the pen's nib had been any harder, I would have gouged holes in the paper.

When I finished writing I sat at the breakfast bar and read back through the outline of my speech. It was good, like *really* good; life-changing, ground-breaking, glass-ceiling-smashing good. It was important, and progressive, maybe too progressive for the likes of the Caine Reynolds partners, but it needed to be said. I was only sorry I couldn't deliver my speech at the Oscars, instead of wasting this beauty at the CRAPs.

I needed to it to show Niamh, and right now. Also, perhaps I needed a cigarette, even though I don't smoke.

I ran upstairs and rinsed the conditioner from my hair, hastily dressed in my favourite mom-jeans and shirt, and got in the car. I drummed my fingers against the steering wheel, waiting as the garage door lifted. *Come on, come on.*

"What are you doing here? It's Friday," said Niamh, blinking at me in my casual clothes.

"I've finished my speech. Read it." I thrust the piece of paper into her hand.

Niamh frowned down at the paper. The poor quality of the ink and my breakneck scribbles had no doubt made it pretty difficult for her to decipher, but I watched Niamh's eyes as they flicked from side to side, growing larger and larger. She finished reading and looked at me, her eyes like moons, and her mouth agog.

"Did you like it?" I said, starting to panic slightly as Niamh had not said anything yet.

"Did you write this on your own, Jaime? It's brilliant!

Wow! I mean… It's incredible. They will *have* to consider you for the position. How can they not? They'd be stupid if they didn't."

I took a deep inhale and smiled. "Phew, thanks."

"You'll knock their socks off. What are you going to wear?"

"I was thinking of going up the Bullring this afternoon – you working? Wanna come?"

"Oh, I can't, I've got...something on this afternoon... but WhatsApp me a picture of what you get, OK? How are you getting there on Friday? Do you want to get ready at mine? Like old times!"

"I have...plans for the day. Oh my gosh, let me tell you."

So I did. I told Niamh all about the following Friday, and how the moms from the group were banding together to help me get the bastard arrested.

"So we'll meet at midday at the race track, corner him, convince him to hand himself in – I can even drive him to the station if necessary – and then we should be back in enough time to get ready for the CRAPs. If not I can drive straight there."

"Why don't you just call the police when you see him at the races?"

Urgh. That's what Erin thought we should do too. I looked at Niamh with the same expression I give when River's shat and it's not my turn to change the nappy.

"OK, OK. You really think you can talk him into handing himself in?"

"Why not? This is what I trained for: convincing people, right? I'm very good at it; you've read my speech."

"Can't argue with that." She laughed and shrugged her shoulders, but her smile dropped almost instantly.

"If that doesn't work then I do have a plan B"

"And what's plan B?"

"Hmm, it's probably best that you don't know." I shuffled my feet. "I'm not sure how legal it is. Anyway... I'd better go, I need to go dress shopping."

"Ooh can I take a copy of your speech?"

"Sure. Actually, I'll come with you to the admin office. I need to use the printer, and I need to ...borrow some supplies from the stationery cupboard."

I picked River up from nursery at one. The nursery worker delighted in regaling me with the details of my daughter's cutlery-wielding abilities. *Hmph*. She never does that at home, eats yogurt with her fingers, but whatever. Then I headed to the Bullring. Friday afternoon, still term time, so shouldn't be too horrendously busy. Not like the weekend.

I parked the car – in a parent and child space: win – and pushed River in her buggy into the mall. I stopped outside the windows of the first clothes shop I came to. It was new. I think. It's been a while since I went out to buy things that aren't food or nappies. Six-foot-high, eye-watering neon letters spelled out the shop's name: Mesh!!! With three exclamation points! The window display was littered with plastic shiny crap; a life-size glittering plastic tiger, a metallic flamingo, and a fucking polar bear vied for window space with mannequins who were all wearing lurid green or pink wigs and sequined gowns, plus there were disco balls, giant monstera leaves and weird square shelves bearing shoes and bags and jewellery, all shiny. It looked like the Great Pacific Garbage Patch had been to the discotech. David Attenborough would probably weep himself to death at the very sight of this place.

Everything in the window seemed to be screaming at me: run away, run away! But there was some kind of magnetic force pulling my attention into the shop, and the more I resisted the stronger the pull became, the need to see what other plastic horrors lay within.

I placated the nagging feeling by telling myself that River would particularly enjoy the sensory assault; after all why pay £5.50 for a baby sensory class when we could just come here.

The inside of the shop, however, was much less ridiculous than the window display, but a quick once over told me that I would find nothing to my tastes. Perhaps maybe fifteen years ago. Though, out of politeness, and because the shop assistants were loitering within visual range, I would pretend to look at the clothes for a few minutes, before making my escape.

"Can I help you with anything?" said a soft voice from behind me. I was feigning interest in a Lycra catsuit with a picture of a leopard's face on the crotch.

"No thank you, I'm just browsing," I replied as I turned around to look at the sales assistant.

Holy shit! Those eyebrows. They were square! And black! Of all the shapes in the world you could draw your eyebrows, why in God's name would you pick square? I blinked several times; maybe it was just a trick of the light, this place was rather dark. The sales assistant, who obviously had a name but there was no way on earth I could move my eyes downwards to read the tag, moved back ever so slightly out of the shadows. They were still there. If anything, they looked bigger in the light. I couldn't look directly at them; she'd know. But like the flapping cock and balls of a halftime streaker, they drew the eye. It was impossible *not* to look at them.

"What are you looking for today?" said Eyebrows.

Shit, an open-ended question. I'm screwed.

I forced myself, with great difficulty, to look at Eyebrows' name tag: Ashley.

"Uh…" Was there any way I could avoid answering her question? Probably not.

Come on Jaime, remember your speech, stop being such a walkover. Just make your excuses and fuck off.

"Uh… Uh…I have a work thing next week and I need a new dress."

Failed.

"Sure, no problem. I can help you find something. Tell me a bit about your work thing."

As it happened, Ashley Eyebrows turned out to be very helpful, and thoughtful. After I had finished explaining the premise of the CRAPs, Ashley instructed me to go to the disabled changing room – to fit the buggy – and she would return with a few items that she thought were suitable.

I stood in front of the mirror, stripped naked except for my trusty giant black pants and my non-wired, non-padded, non-supportive of any kind, saggy AF, breast-feeding bra. I stood side on, and let my eyes follow the curve of my tummy. What was once concave, now stuck out and hung down over the top of my pants like a stripy, deflated balloon.

I ran my fingers over the top. My C-section scar and stretch marks were still tingly to the touch. Would that last forever? I squished the tops of my thighs; they were definitely bigger, dimplier, more gelatinous than before I got pregnant, and there were dark patches of skin appearing in the middles where they rubbed together. This was the first time in ages that I had surveyed my new mom body properly – we don't have any full-length mirrors at home, for no other reason than I've never found one I really liked. A voice at the back of my mind told me that I should be hating my new body; that was the done thing. The magazines would be full of advice on how to 'fix' it, make it smaller, less lumpy, whiter… but actually I don't mind it. No scratch that; I like it! I guess that makes me a rebel. But just feel how soft my tummy is! It feels like a proved lump of bread dough, just before it's about to go in the oven. And I love bread. I looked at River in the mirror. She was dribbling and laughing back at me.

I whispered to her, "One day I'll teach you how not to give any fu—.

"Are you ready?" Ashley Eyebrows said through the curtain.

"Yep." I stopped caressing my belly and looked up.

The curtain jerked sideways and Ashley stepped inside the fitting room, her arms full of gowns. I had momentarily forgotten the sheer scale of the eyebrows but was surprised to find that I drew comfort from seeing them again.

"The first dress I thought you could try is this one." She held a long, pink dress aloft, one arm holding the hanger and the other, like a bar, pushing the waist of the gown forward. "It's a rare Rueberry original, sunset ombre, fully sequinned, fluted hem. I thought with your dark skin tone and your figure you could really pull off this colour and cut."

Half-dubious, half-giddy with excitement, I took the dress from Ashley, who helped me to step into it and then zipped it up at the back. This was princess level dress-up.

"You'll need to take your bra off for this dress," said Ashley, stepping back into the curtain to take in all my form.

"I can't. I'm still breastfeeding. I'll leak everywhere."

"Hmm." Ashley placed her hands on her hips. "You'll have to use stick on pads. Do you have any of those?"

"No."

"It's not a problem, you can get them from Boots. If you get this dress, I'll give you a roll of tit tape as well just to make extra sure the pads are stuck down."

"Ok, thanks."

After faffing a bit with the bra area, and failing to make my bulky, shapeless uniboob look a bit more flattering, I took a step back and gazed at my magnificent reflection. I was so shiny. I turned from side to side, the bottom of the dress swishing mesmerically. It was as if the dress had been made to measure. It perfectly outlined my waist and hips, and seemed to add curves where Instagram told me that curves should be. It was very sparkly, though. Maybe too sparkly for the CRAPs. Wait – could anything be too sparkly? I swayed on the spot, my eyes unfocused in the glittery reflections of the sequins. It was like a teeny firework display in the fitting room.

"It's fancier than my wedding dress," I said.

"You look like a mermaid," said Ashley. She was watching my face rather than the dress.

"Yes. I do," I smiled. "How much is it?"

"That dress is £495."

"Pounds?!"

"It's on sale. Marked down from £1200."

"Hmm. What else have you got?"

"Oh plenty, actually," said Ashley, a slight tinge of disappointment in her voice.

Later that day I dragged the shopping bags, River's car seat, and a dry cleaners-style dress bag into the house.

Once I got River bathed and in bed, with relatively little drama for a change, I rescued the almost undrunk glass of Kaluha from the bathroom and headed downstairs.

I pulled the clothes bag out from under the stairs where I'd stashed it earlier, and hung it up in front of the TV. In slow motion, savouring each inch, I unzipped the bag. Sitting back on the couch, I took a sip of my drink and gazed at the bag's contents.

This is the best show I've ever seen, I thought, as the light from a million ombre pink sequins danced around my living room.

"Morning Ryan," I said, on Monday at 8 a.m.

In response, Ryan swivelled his chair in the opposite direction, so he was facing away from me.

"Okay, that's fine," I muttered to myself. I placed my handbag under the table and tapped my fingers against my knees.

There was something I was supposed to do today...

"Oh yeah!" I lunged forward and grabbed the phone receiver. "Do you know the number for HR?" I said to Ryan's back.

That was it. I was going to take back control of my own career and life, starting with getting HR to send through my forms and training schedule, and then getting promoted to partner.

Ryan stood up and, still ignoring me, strode out of the office, walking past an incoming Rachel.

"Morning, Jaime. Clive asked if you could see him in his office?" she said, throwing down the mornings post on the desk.

"What does he want now?" My fingers poised over the buttons.

Rachel shrugged. "No idea, sorry." She carried on with her post round.

I hung the receiver back on the handset. I couldn't remember the number for HR anyway – I'd have to look it up on the intranet and I need HR to reset my passwords for that. *Ugh*, it was a vicious circle. I sighed, smoothed down my skirt, and made my way to Clive's office.

His door was ajar. I was just about to knock when I spotted that he was on the phone so I stopped myself, fist held up in mid-air.

Clive saw me and made a beckoning gesture with his hand. Once inside, he put his hand over the mouthpiece and whispered, "Sit down".

I obliged.

I clocked the mutilated corner of the desk that I had shambolically tried to fix a few days ago. The paper had vanished, but the other elements of the atrocious repair job remained in place.

I watched Clive listening on the phone for a few minutes, maybe it was even a decade. His expression was similar to the one that I had worn a few months ago when I had endured thirty solid minutes of my eight-year-old nephew detailing all the names he had given to his fifty million Ratattas, and where he had caught them. And then I remembered that Clive's eyes can sometimes not look in the same direction, and, wait, was he looking at me this whole time?

I hastily looked down at my interlocking fingers. Clive hung up the phone.

"Conference call with the partners," he said, his eyes now definitely looking in my direction.

I didn't have anything to say to that, so I just nodded.

"Right so, do you want the bad news or the good news first?"

"Bad." Better to be prepared, save the good news as a treat.

"Now, there's some sort of technical issue with the files in HR, so that's why your return-to-work forms have been delayed. But, I'm promised that they will have them ready for you to sign by Friday at the latest." Clive held his finger up to stop me from interrupting, not that I was going to. "Your reassessment training. I've got a list of the things here that you will need to redo; most of it is just stuff like manual-handling and fire safety, but the actual assessments we can't do until HR get their systems fixed. I've spoken to IT and they've said it could be a few weeks or even a couple of months yet."

"What's the problem? Is it with the files or the system?" I wasn't sure that I was following.

"Uh..." He scratched his temple. "Yes."

Right that clears it up.

He held his finger up again. "Now the good news."

I sat back in the chair, my shoulders relaxing a little. Hopefully this would be worth it.

"We've had an email. It arrived on Friday morning, from Mrs. Montgomery. She absolutely gushed about you. Boy, did she like you. Her husband, Don Montgomery, was one of our *most* prestigious clients. She was so enamoured with you and how you handled everything that she has recommended you to all of her – equally wealthy – friends. In fact, your name, well, not yours in particular, but Caine Reynolds, came up on the course over the weekend. They have a ladies session on a Thursday and apparently we were the hot topic." He was practically rubbing his hands together. "So the partners and I have had a chat, and we are happy for you to continue working with the high-profile clients."

This would explain Ryan's shitty mood.

"Great, that's excellent, thanks," I said. "Will I get my office back?"

"Uhh, not just yet. You're not legally allowed to sign your name off."

I really ought to double-check whether I need to have my training up to date to write wills, or whether it's just Caine Reynolds' policy.

"So you'll still be working with Ryan for the meantime."

"But... So wait, I have to do all the work and Ryan gets his name stamped at the bottom of all my correspondence? Is that what you're saying?"

"At least you'll actually be working and not just fannying about on reception with your knickers on show. Look, it'll only be for a little while until HR get their problems fixed. You can continue doing what you do best, and Caine Reynolds gets a whole heap of new clients, it's win-win."

Was it a win? If it was why did I feel so icky?

Come on Jaime, take control, tell him to sort the paperwork now.

I looked down at the bodged desk corner again. "Ok well... I get my own desk. I don't want to share with Ryan anymore."

Ugh. It was a start.

"Sure, anything else?" His eyes crinkled at the corners.

Do it, say it now.

"And uh... I... uh... I want one of those nice chairs with the head rests."

He scrutinised me for a second. I felt like a graduate again. Sitting in this office with freshly-washed hair and a polyester skirt-suit, waiting to start my first day of training.

"No problem darling. I'll put in the order with admin later today." He nodded towards the door; this was my dismissal.

I stood up and made to leave.

"Wait a sec," he said, and I turned around hopefully. "You couldn't do me a favour could you? I've had some expen— I mean customised clubs made, they'll be ready on Friday, I need you to pick them up for me, you can bring them to the award ceremony. I would do it myself but I'm working in the daytime and you're not, and you live right by Greenvale club, right?"

"Eh…"

Of course, I couldn't tell him about the vigilante criminal hunting mission I had planned for that day.

"I might," he began, noticing that I was probably searching for a way to say no, "be able to sort something out with IT to get your assessments done quicker."

It sounded an awful lot like bribery to me, but I couldn't tell him about Rob and I was unable to think of another excuse as to why I couldn't pick up his clubs, and I really just wanted to get my licenses sorted.

"What time does the golf club open?"

The rest of the week passed without much provocation. Ryan was still cold-shouldering me, both a blessing and also really fucking annoying, especially when we had to correlate schedules and share client meetings. Niamh had been practicing a phony acceptance speech on the joke promise that I would read out her name on Friday regardless of what the envelope said. Marie had been moved to a different safe house. She had her own kitchen and bathroom now. She said that Rob had turned up at her mum's house one afternoon and broke the front door off its hinges, but otherwise she hadn't heard anything about him.

The police still hadn't arrested him, though thankfully he had not paid me, nor any of the other moms a visit. Although saying that, I swear I saw him a few times during my rounds with River; there was a man at the bus stop outside of the swimming pool, a navy jersey jacket zipped up to his chin, and the same man again at the corner of Gloucester Road, where we went for Baby Sign, and then outside of the library, on Thursday where I took River to her story session. It was probably just someone that looked like him to be fair. Your mind can play tricks like that, and I haven't even really seen him in real life, just in photographs and on the CCTV screen.

The police had also failed to chase us up regarding the appearance of Rob at Caine Reynolds. We – mostly Niamh – were expecting a visit during the week, Rachel had even prepared CDs with CCTV footage for them, but nothing, not a single officer. Maybe Marie was right, and they just didn't care. Niamh pointed out that they probably didn't have the resources these days.

Jaime Wright - 12th March - 21:56
 Any news today on Rob?

Erin Schellenger - 12th March - 21:59
 No arrests yet. We still on for tomorrow?

Jaime Wright - 12th March - 22:02

Def. See you at midday at the racetrack. Don't forget to wear your fancy clobber.

Carys Honeyman - 12th March - 22:09
See you there. Can't wait to meet you all.

Kelly Vaughan - 12th March - 22:13
See you tomorrow. So excited. I've got the stuff you asked for.

CHAPTER FIVE

"Hi, I'm here to pick up some golf clubs."

The man behind the counter looked me up and down. At this precise moment in time I was sporting jeans, a Hufflepuff hoodie and a very, very messy mom-bun, that without seeing in the mirror, I could at least pretend was cute.

"What's the name?" he said in a sharp nasal voice. He pursed his lips together, making them disappear entirely. He was a little man, short and slight, and very old. He had a tiny spattering of wispy blonde hair and the faintest husks of eyebrows and eyelashes. He looked a bit like a naked mole rat. I had seen them at the zoo one time. Weird-looking things. They looked like dicks.

"Clive Ross." I checked the clock behind the counter: 10:05 a.m.

"Hmm, not for you then?" he said, but he didn't wait for me to answer before disappearing out the back.

How long would this take? I needed to get ready. The drive to Wolverhampton would only take thirty minutes so long as there weren't any road works or race traffic, but I still needed to shower, defuzz, put on make-up, do my hair, and put on my dress.

The shop was small and dark, and overwhelmingly crammed with golfing stuff; clothing, balls, clubs and other colourful little things I was only moderately intrigued by. I ran my fingers over a row of clubs next to the counter. Why couldn't Clive just pick one of these clubs? I could have collected it and be gone already. This one is £150! *Pfft*. What a waste of money. £150 for a stick. I glanced at the clock again: 10:08.

Naked Mole Rat man came back into the shop carrying two long, thin boxes, and smiling as though he held the world's greatest treasure in his hands and could not wait for me to join in with the excitement.

He set the boxes on the glass counter and began to open one, agonisingly slowly. It was like some kind of weird strip-tease. He slid a box opener that was attached to his lanyard down the centre slit, through the branded parcel tape, and slowly peeled back the box flaps.

10:15. *FML*.

He removed the black tissue paper, stamped with a slick silver logo, and folded it carefully, placing it to one side. Inside was a long velvet pouch bearing the same logo. He took the bag out and carefully slid back the velvet sheath.

Fuck's sake. 10.18. It's taken him three bloody minutes to get that bastard stick out of the bag.

Finally, he held the naked club in his hands, and caressing the head, he presented it to me in a similar manner that the midwife had handed River to Olly once she had been cut from me, weighed, and wrapped in a blanket. His eyes were glowing.

"This is a Vailingtons Graphite X419 Pro Bullet Finish Custom Fit Irons," he said, in his best M&S ad impression.

"Okie dokie. Do I need to sign anything?"

Naked Mole Rat Man, who already seemed somewhat crumpled by life, appeared to fold inwards on himself. Obviously not the reaction he was hoping for, and I did feel a little guilty, but he was seriously eating into my shaving time. He passed me a tablet thingy to sign my name on and then wrapped the club back up in the velvet bag and tissue paper, and gently placed it back in the box, as though he was laying a dearly beloved pet to rest.

"Would you like to see the other one?" It was clear that the still-unwrapped club was his preference of the two, and why he had planned to save the unveiling for last, but his eyes had given up all their sparkle.

"No thank you," I smiled. 10:22.

I scooped up the boxes and Naked Mole Rat Man handed me the invoice.

"Wow, £3985 on golf clubs!" I gave a long whistle. "Bostin' mate, see ya."

Nearly £4k on shiny sticks, yet the shittest desk in the whole building. Go figure.

My car has one of those really cool boot things where you wave your foot underneath and it opens automatically. I threw the clubs in the back. Naked Mole Rat Man watched from the window, his head barely visible among the DIY shop information signs. As I pulled away I thought I saw him shake his head and wipe his cheek.

At 10:45, I pulled into the empty garage, and pelted up the stairs, undressing as I went.

I scrubbed my face, possibly a little too roughly, and washed my hair with speedy ferocity. I had planned on doing the full defuzzing routine in preparation for tonight's events, but that weird dick rodent had taken way more time that I had anticipated. What with his perverse club unsheathing and all. I would have to settle for shaving only my shins. Considering they were the only parts of my legs on show, I supposed it didn't really matter that the rest of my legs looked a bit like the furry cactus we had in the kitchen that Olly's auntie Donna bought us. I almost forgot about the pitts, but remembered at the last minute. I didn't bother with the bush.

I scraped the towel against my skin then I dried my hair as quickly as I could in front of the mirror, the towel now wrapped around me like a dress. I rubbed foundation onto my face and quickly put on mascara, blusher and then drew on my eyebrows. I am old enough to have lived through the skinny eyebrows trend of the nineties and had, unfortunately, and permanently, lost the best part of my brows to over-plucking.

I sat back and regarded my handiwork in the mirror. That would have to do.

If the thing with Rob went to plan, I could always come back home and finish getting ready properly before heading to the CRAPs, but if it did not, I could go straight to the ceremony from the racecourse. As it was a fancy cup event, everyone should be wearing their finest clothes. My Rueberry original was perhaps too fancy, too glittery, for a day at the races, but fuck it, I didn't spend almost 400 quid on a dress to wear it only once to a crummy work's party.

After sellotaping pads onto my boobs like Ashley Eyebrows showed me, I pooled the dress onto the carpet like a big doughnut and stepped into the hole, wiggling my hips as I pulled it up by the straps. I bent over slightly so that I could see most of the gown in the dresser mirror. I looked pretty good. I winked at myself, though I couldn't actually see it because my head was cut off in the reflection.

I stood up straight and sashayed to the bedroom door, my hands caressing the sequins on my hips. It was heavy and a bit scratchy, but I felt positively regal. If there had been anyone to languidly wave towards, I would have.

The sequins crunched on the leather car seat. Thank God it was only a thirty minute drive. I took my heels off and threw them onto the passenger seat, along with my clutch bag and a pink fascinator left over from my cousin's wedding last year.

My stomach churned. Butterflies. I was going to cement the capture of a wanted criminal. Sure, that was exciting and a little nerve-wracking, but why did I feel as though I was going on a first date?

I thought of the other moms I would be seeing today: Erin the vlogger, originally from America but now lives in an idyllic lakeside cottage in the Cotswolds; Carys from Wrexham, so kind-hearted, and always posting useless diet tips that I so often 'liked' without reading; and Kelly, from Derby, PTSD and PND survivor and prolific poster of Harry Potter memes. I had never met them before in real life but I knew everything about them, absolutely everything; which moms have piles; which moms secretly hate their MILs, which ones' husbands never do any housework, but this is the first time we would actually meet face to face.

Oh God. I hope they like me.

I pulled up to the racecourse car park at midday exactly and clutched the steering wheel, trying to steady my breathing before I got out of the car. My heart was fluttering in my chest and adrenaline was beginning to leaden my arms and legs. I could not say for sure if I was more nervous to meet the wanted criminal, and try and talk him into handing himself in, or to meet a few women I knew from the internet. A few wonderful women whom I had come to consider near family. My hands trembled slightly as I opened the car door.

From the passenger seat I grabbed my fascinator and jammed it onto my head. I put my shoes back on, snatched my clutch bag up, and stepped out of the car, looking around for signs of the other moms. Would I recognise them? I had only seen photos of them before. We did Selfie Saturdays, so I was pretty sure I knew what they looked like, but what if they'd changed their hair or they looked different in their frocks? What if I ended up hanging around the carpark all day in a ridiculously heavy, itchy dress? OMG, what if they ghosted me?

"JAIME!" From nowhere came a rib-crushing hug. The person squeezing the life out of me released me and took a step back. I was flooded with relief and excitement. I definitely recognised the hug-giver. It was Erin. She held me out at arm's length and drank in my appearance.

"Wow hun, you look amazing!" she said.

"So do you!" Erin was wearing a knee-length, green wrap dress, shiny silver sandals and an enormous satellite dish of a hat that was perched on the side of her head.

"I cannot believe it has taken this long for us all to meet," she smiled. She looked off to the left, and there stood Carys.

Younger than both Erin and myself, Carys was wearing a bright red dress, and she had long ginger hair and pillar-box coloured lips – she looked like some sort of fifties pin up.

"Helloo." She gave a small close-to-the-body wave that said 'I'm very happy to meet you but I'm not a hugger'. Erin pulled her into another rib-cracker regardless.

"Just waiting for Kelly now," I said, looking around the car park.

"I think that's her," mumbled Carys. She pointed near the far end where we could see the figure of a woman in a lilac dress, crouching over, picking something off the bottom of her shoe maybe. She clocked us and waved frantically, dropping her bag at the same time, the contents littering the gravel.

"Lovely day for catching criminals," said Erin, looking up at the crisp blue sky.

"I'm actually really excited. I've never done anything like this before," said Carys in her Welsh accent. From her expression you wouldn't know she was excited – in fact it looked like she might barf.

We watched Kelly grow closer and closer, she was watching her feet as she walked, every few metres she would look up and wave madly again.

"Oh my god, you're all real!" she said when she finally got within earshot. She ran the last few feet to us; a feat, which in those heels and on this gravel, would have been difficult for anyone, but for Kelly seemed insurmountable. She held the skirt of her dress up in the crook of her arm. This proved, almost instantly, to be a good idea, when her foot found a natural dip in the gravel and she went crashing down to the ground, her knees slamming hard into the stones.

"I'm okay," she laughed, jumping back to her feet. "I'm just nervous." Her knees were cut, and a few stones were still stuck to them. She brushed them off, and then spat on her fingers and rubbed the cuts. "It's fine," she said taking in our expressions, "happens all the time." I spotted yellowing bruises across her shins and knees. She dropped the skirt of her dress instantly covering them.

Erin launched at her and gave her a huge hug, and so did I. Carys leaned in for a millisecond. We were all grinning.

"I can't believe we're finally meeting," I said, taking in their faces. These faces that I knew so well. How could I have ever thought that I wouldn't recognise them? It was like thinking I wouldn't recognise my sister. Though actually, given my sister's propensity for injecting Playdoh or whatever the trend was these days into her lips, that could be a very real prospect soon.

"So, what's the plan?" said Erin, and all three women looked at me.

I guess I'm in charge now. Probably not the best idea, but Niamh's not here to dispute it.

"I already have the tickets." I held up my bag. "So, we just need to get in the grounds and then find Rob. Do you remember what he looked like?"

They all nodded.

"And then we'll just chat to him. I honestly believe that on some level he must feel a little bit guilty for what he has done, surely. Marie always said he felt terrible every time he did it and that she never believed any of it was his fault, it was just his temper. If we can convince him to hand himself in, then he could get proper counselling, or pills, or whatever he needs you know? And hopefully if he's in prison for a bit, then Marie can come out of hiding."

They nodded again, but this time slower and with a few side glances at each other.

"And if that fails then we have plan B," I said.

Kelly looked at me, winked, and gave me one of those finger gun salutes.

"Right, ready?" I said.

"Ready," said Erin, and she hooked her arm into the crook of Carys'.

"Ready," said Carys, looking at her arm and then smiling at Erin.

"Hang on..." said Kelly, and she gathered her skirt up once more. "Ready."

The four of us swept into the entrance tunnel of the grounds. I flashed the tickets at a nearby neon-vested ticket checker and we sauntered past. If it was a movie, this part would have been in slow motion, with some cool bassy music playing, and some wind turbines on us. And then I would take off my Raybans and swish my hair.

We emanated at the other end of the tunnel, looking magnificent in our rainbow of frocks, the sunlight immediately attacking our eyes. I have this thing called photic sneeze reflex, so obviously I launched into a sneezing fit. I had to stop walking and cross my legs tight, because I'd had a baby only nine months ago and, although she was an emergency sun-roof baby, nine months of continuous bladder and cervical pressure had left my pelvic floor shot to fuck, and I had been seriously neglecting my 'special' exercises.

"Bless you," said Erin.

Once inside, and once my sneezing was under control, we looked up and down the patrons' area beside the track. It was huge. So big, in fact, that we couldn't see either end. It looked as though we might have been somewhere in the middle of the race viewing section, but it was impossible to tell. To the right we could see stacked covered seating, rising up to a few storeys high. To the left there were lawns and people, just crowds and crowds of people, and hats, so many hats. And everywhere there were men stood next to podiums with huge signs bearing names of horses and numbers next to them like 8/1 or 110/1.

I looked from left to right and back again – no sign of Rob. It was like we were watching tennis, not waiting for the races to start. All the women attendees were wearing fine dresses. Any worries I had of being overdressed quickly vanished; I fitted right in. You'd never know I was a race virgin. Most of the men were wearing morning suits and top hats. Damn, it was going to be hard to find him.

"Where do we start?" said Carys, chewing her thumb nail.

"I say we start with a drink," said Kelly, and with just a slight nod from Erin, she was off, skirt hooked over her arm, stomping towards the nearest bar. She returned only moments later carrying a bottle of fizz in one hand and four plastic champagne flutes in the other.

Probably, by the time I needed to drive again the alcohol would have worn off, so I held out my hand for a glass like the other moms.

Kelly stuck the bottle between her legs and began pulling at the cork. "Here's to…"

"Friendship?" said Carys.

BANG.

The cork flew out of the top with the sound of gunfire, soared thirty or so feet into the air, and in a tremendous arc landed on some woman's shiny blonde head. The woman smoothed her hair and glanced up at the sky. Fizzy wine erupted from Kelly's hand, and she raced to fill up each glass with the fountain.

"To friendship," I said, holding my glass in the centre of the gap we made. "And to ForumFriends groups."

"And to vigilante justice," said Erin.

"To vigilante justice," we chimed with a laugh, knocking our glasses together in the circle.

I took a sip, the bubbles tingling inside my mouth and down my neck. Mmm… tasted like indigestion, but it was worth it to be here with my friends.

I briefly thought of the only person in the world that I considered my real life friend, Niamh, and a pang hit me in the stomach. Was it guilt? I imagined her at work, mindlessly typing away on her keyboard, her rich tea biscuit accidentally falling into her lukewarm tea after dunking for a nanosecond too long. I've been a pretty shit friend recently.

I'll fix that tonight though.

"Let's have your choices then please ladies," came a low, loud, Yorkshire accent from behind us. It belonged to one of the independent bookies on the grounds.

I shook my head, "Oh we're not actually here to bet."

"What are you doing at the Royal Spring Cup then? If you're not here to bet?"

The moms and I exchanged smirks.

"Come on ladies, it's part of the fun, you're not having a good time unless you've got a flutter on. Who will it be?"

I don't know why, but I've always had a slightly uneasy feeling about horse racing. Was it cruel? I wasn't even sure. It's not as if I was an animal activist or anything; Niamh's the vegan, not me. I looked at the bookie, and then at the other moms. I definitely thought I heard one of them say "when in Rome."

"Um, okay, I'll do a tenner on Drug Of Choice," said Kelly stepping forward with her cash in her hand.

"To win or each way?" said the bookie.

"To win," said Kelly, with a 'well, duh' expression.

I had no idea what this meant.

"Five, please, for me on Criminal Minds," said Erin, with a wink towards me. "Each way," she added before the bookie could ask.

"I'll do five also on… Um… on Just The Ticket, to win," said Carys, flipping her beautiful hair over her shoulder and handing him the cash.

"And you, love, what will you choose?" he said to me.

I looked at the board. The names of the horses all smushed together. *Agh*. I couldn't read them fast enough – I was taking too long to decide. And then I saw a name at the very bottom, and I knew that was the horse I wanted.

"Lucky Day please."

"How much?"

"Ten please." I only had ten-pound notes. Do bookies even give change?

"And do you want to win or each way?"

Oh God. "Uh… To win?"

"Very nice, I like your style, all or nothing. That one's two hundred to one as well, so if he wins you'll be in for a nice little packet."

Fuck.

I didn't know much about horse racing, but I knew, with unwavering certainty, that 200/1 meant a really shit horse. Maybe it was a brand-new baby horse, or maybe a really old one. Maybe this was its last ride, before it was made into lasagne. I felt uneasy again. The champagne bubbles seemed to be popping in my neck. I took the slip from the bookie and stuffed it into the small inside pocket of my clutch bag.

"Guys! Oh my god look down there!" Carys was pointing down to the right by the row of stands. At the very front, leaning against the white railings was, even at this distance, the unmistakable bulldog tattoo of Rob Sparks.

The crowds of finely-dressed attendees grew denser and more excitable the closer we got to the stands, and to Rob. We had to weave in and out of groups of people, occasionally only narrowly avoiding knocking drinks or betting slips out of people's hands. I did not believe it was possible to say "sorry" so often in such a short span of time.

Looking back over my shoulder, I saw huge swathes of empty lawn littered with unoccupied plastic chairs. These people could sit there, why had they all clambered into the same space? What was so great about the stands?

Eventually the moms and I managed to find a spot somewhere around the middle, about five rows up from the bottom. If you drew a line from us to the finish line of the track, it would pass right through Rob and his party.

I stared at the back of Rob's – probably rented – top hat. He was with at least four other men all wearing exactly the same grey suits and holding plastic pint glasses filled with beer or cider. They looked like a wedding party. Lads' day out at the races. One of them, the one on the far right of the group, was very probably Rob's brother, Bradley. They had the same slightly-too-short noses, same wide-rounded shoulders, and the same heavy-to-the-right gait.

We wouldn't be able to make our move with the other men around. I needed him alone, without backup. I hadn't thought about what we would do if we couldn't get him alone. Maybe we could just wait for him to go to the loo, or the bar.

The crowd became so dense that eventually it was too difficult to chat with the other moms. Yet, Rob's harsh bark of a laugh carried up to us, over all the noise, every few moments. It was like a sinister tick-tock on some countdown clock. How many more beats would we get before our challenge time was up?

The moms and I communicated to each other mostly using expressions, eyebrow movements, and occasionally mouthing the odd short sentence like "there's five races today" and "first race in ten minutes".

"WE SHOULD JUST CALL THE POLICE NOW," said Erin over the top of the noise, but even her shouts were drowned out by the sheer volume; there would be no way we could hold a phone conversation with the emergency services. I was inwardly glad.

The crowd eventually began to quiet, and a readiness stirred. It was an ebbing wave. I squinted down to the front of the track where I could barely make out the blur of the starting blocks.

BANG!

Another champagne cork. No – this time actual gunfire, amplified through the sound system and echoing through the grounds. A Mexican wave of overwhelming noise spread through the stands, starting at the far end and swiftly growing nearer. Men and women were besides themselves, screaming hysterically, waving their bits of paper, like thousands of tiny white flags. A hundred hooves smashed the mud and a rainbow flashed in front of my eyes.

And, as abruptly as it had started, it was over. A low hum of murmuring now filled the void, with sporadic cheers. We waited all that time for less than a minute of excitement.

Of course, my horse came last.

"I won, I won," said Carys, stiffly jumping up and down.

"Ooh, how much did you win?" asked Kelly.

"Um, about £250 I think. It was fifty to one."

Erin high-fived Carys. "Nice."

The crowds began moving in every which way. Some flocked to the bars, others to the bathroom, and the lucky ones with winning slips in their hands headed back to the bookies where they'd placed their original bets. Carys looked down the track to the Yorkshire guy we betted with, and sighed. He seemed really far away now.

"Here, I'll come with you," said Erin, hooking Carys' arm once again. She looked at Kelly and me and said,

"You two wait here and keep your eye on *that.*" She nodded towards the back of Rob's head, "and call us if he's on the move."

"Yep will do," I said, patting the bulge my phone made in my clutch bag, just to make sure it was still there.

But Rob didn't move, and it looked like none of his party had chosen that particular horse, or needed refills or pees, because they all stayed, steadfast, in their prime race-watching spot.

"Do you want another drink?" said Kelly after a while. "I think I might get a G&T."

"I'm driving so I don't think I will, plus I need a clear head to think, but you get one. I'll have a coke if you go to the bar, thanks."

Then Kelly left me to guard not only Rob and his gang, but our spot in the stands. As the minutes ticked on, I found it more and more difficult to defend a big enough space for all four of us. I was getting jostled and pushed from all sides. Peoples' backs and handbags slowly depressed the gap. Hopefully the other moms could expand it again. Where were they?

My boobs were beginning to get pretty full, and the straps of my gown were starting to cut into my chest. Oh shit, they might be leaking. I looked down – it was OK, the sequins had hid any leaks.

Carys and Erin were the first to arrive back. They looked nonplussed at the much smaller gap for them to stand in but didn't pass comment on it, thankfully.

"Where's Kelly?" said Erin looking around.

"She's at the bar," I said.

Carys looked in the general direction of the nearest bar, possibly to see if Kelly was on her way back. "Is she the one with the drinking problem?"

Erin and I exchanged looks. The answer was obvious

to anyone who had been on the moms' group for as long as we had, but it felt wrong to say it aloud. Erin opened her mouth to speak—

"Excuse me love." Came a voice from behind. A man in his early twenties attempted to shimmy through the gap between us and the next row of seats but he guffed it spectacularly and sent Carys flying forwards a few feet, her clutch bag catapulted out of her hands and her newly collected winnings rained down upon the rows in front like in the last bit of the Crystal Maze.

"Oh no!" she shouted

"I'm so sorry!" said the man, his face beetroot red. He immediately ran forward, probably with the intention of helping Carys to gather her money, but instead he knocked into several other people, causing a huge commotion. People began laughing. I felt wretched for him, but before I could extend my sympathies, he legged it.

A few honest race-goers were passing Carys notes they had grabbed out of the air. I took a tenner from someone two rows in front. As I looked down the line of the seats, my eyes swept to the left. Rob was staring directly at me.

I turned around on the spot, my back to him so that he could no longer see my face.

"What's up?" said Erin, in a serious voice, after spotting the sudden change in my behaviour.

"He saw me. Rob. He looked right at me."

"God, really? Do you think he recognised you?" said Carys, completely abandoning her attempts to recollect the money. The few people who were still holding notes aloft gave up waiting and pocketed the cash.

"I don't know. He had a look on his face like 'I know you but I don't know where from.' Is he still looking?"

Erin inched around me and snuck a look at Rob. Would he recognise her too?

"Yes, he's still looking in this direction. I think he's looking *for* you."

"Fuck."

"What's going on here?" said Kelly, squeezing under the arm of one of the men next to us on the row. She was carrying two fizzing drinks in plastic cups, a clear one and a black one. She handed the black one to me.

"Rob saw Jaime. We think he might have recognised her and now he's looking for her," Carys said in a stage whisper.

Kelly leaned back and peered through the crook of the same man's elbow. "He's not looking anymore."

My muscles relaxed. I looked over my shoulder. Kelly was right, Rob had turned back around to face the racetrack again. Maybe he had decided that he didn't know me after all. But moments later, we learned the real reason he had turned away from us: the familiar roaring from the crowd rose again, and twelve or a hundred horses thundered in front of our faces to the sounds of grown adults totally losing their shit.

Two races down, three to go. He would need the toilet soon. His glass was empty now – maybe he'd need a refill.

The man was a camel. We watched as he was brought pint after pint by his mates. Where was he storing it all? Surely he must need to pee by now? We stood through another two races, a further hour and a half of waiting for this jerk to do something, anything, on his own. None of us could be bothered to bet again, but Kelly was keen to maintain her supply of alcohol. The rest of us had switched to pop. There was only one race left. Rob had begun to sway, and shout, and sing. He was getting drunk. The plan wasn't going to work. We hadn't accounted for him drinking this much, or at least I'd have thought we'd have handled the matter by now. It was slipping through my fingers.

His friends were laughing and goading him.

"I'll get this one then," he said, his laddish voice carrying up over the crowds in the rows between us, and he turned and walked away from the stands – alone.

Finally!

"This is it!" I shouted, elbowing the other moms who all immediately stood to attention.

"Yes, he's on his own. Quick." Erin ushered us down the row, dodging and ducking through the merry racegoers along the way.

But, by the time we made it to the end of stand, he had vanished.

"Maybe he's peeing," Carys said.

The line for the ladies was about twenty people deep; predictably, there was no line for the gents. He could have easily slipped inside before we got there.

"You two wait here, and Kelly and I will try the bar in case he went there. One-ring us if you see him," I said. I grabbed Kelly's hand and rushed through the marquee doors into the bar area.

The bar was jam-packed with people, desperate to get their drinks in before the last race. Probably not the best idea for everyone it seemed; there were several people in there who'd clearly already had a skinful. One man perched by the entrance had his eyes closed and his hands raving out in front of him, like he was reading an imaginary crystal ball, and there was a blonde woman sitting at the table next to us with her head in her lap.

She looked oddly familiar.

Oh shit, was she the woman we hit with the cork?

Most of the men were no longer wearing their hats – or maybe it was customary to take them off before you go inside, if you could even call this inside. It's more like a big tent.

"There!" said Kelly pointing to the far end. Rob's head was bobbing back through the crowd and his eyes were pointed downwards, towards whatever he was carrying. I got my phone out and rang Erin's number. I kept one eye on Rob's bouncing head, and the other on the screen of my phone. Erin cut off the call, which meant she understood we had seen Rob, and moments later she and Carys joined us in the mouth of the marquee. Just at the exact same moment Rob did.

He was carrying a tray bearing five pints of beer; one of the pints was a few mouthfuls short of being full. He looked up from his tray and spotted us. He smiled.

"I know you!" he laughed. "Where do I know you from?"

Right Jaime you can do this. You're a successful solicitor, you've trained for eight years so that you can reason with people for a living. Boss it.

He was taller than I expected, and bigger, broader. My eyes leapt from the beers on the tray, over his slightly protruding belly, and to his enormous arms in his suit jacket. I thought of Marie, in her room with a nine-month-old baby and, impulsively, I imagined being punched in the face by him; my lip and brow splitting as Marie's had. My hand shot to my mouth, maybe to double-check there was no sutured gash, or maybe to stop words from escaping. My chest felt as though the horses were stampeding down the track again. I just had to remain calm. I could do this.

"Hi, my name's Jaime," I began, my legs began to tremble, my arms felt oddly stiff and heavy, and I was keenly aware of how little my mouth was moving as the words came out. "I'm a friend of—"

His face dropped; his smile vanished in an instant. He knew who I was.

"What's going on?" He looked at each of us in turn. "What has Marie been saying about me?"

I gulped the air and inhaled a mouthful of alcohol and cologne fumes.

"No, no, she hasn't said anything," said Erin, her eyes wide, her gaze flicking between Rob and me, and back to Rob.

"Where is she?" He spat.

"That's not why we're here to talk," I said, forcing myself to keep my voice even. "If we could just chat to you for a mo—"

"Where the FUCK is my wife?!"

I thought he might have thrown the tray of beers at us.

"Please, can we just talk?" I said, but I knew I had lost it. My voice was barely audible over the chatter and clinking in the tent.

"Tell me where she is or get the fuck out of my way," he said. His face was red and blotchy, though his knuckles were white against the black plastic tray. He stepped forward so that the end of it pressed painfully into my rib cage.

"Plan B, plan B!" said Erin in rapid whispers.

"Already done mate," said Kelly, staring Rob square in the eye. She must have been a good seven or eight inches shorter than him, even in her ridiculous heels. She puffed her chest out and stepped to the side. The other moms and I parted to let him walk through.

"I swear to God if you mess with my business again…" He was looking right at me.

I was getting tunnel vision again. I stared at Rob

hoping that words would fall from my mouth, but nothing came.

My plan had failed. It was a shit plan. Niamh was right. I never think things through properly. I obviously wasn't the wordsmith I imagined – I couldn't even string two sentences together let alone convince him to hand himself to the police. Why did I ever think that was a good idea? Why am I still allowed to make plans? I can definitely say goodbye to that partner position. The CRAPs were due to start in only a few hours. How can I deliver a rallying speech, when I can't even speak now? The words were still absent as we watched Rob march out of the marquee.

"Oh my god, are you OK?" Carys said, rushing closer.

Erin put her arm around me. "Don't beat yourself up, I don't think anyone could have convinced him to talk. We still have plan B."

"Did you do it?" I said, turning to Kelly.

She winked. "Of course."

"How did you know which beer was his?" said Erin.

"Because he had already drunk from it," said Kelly with a smile.

We walked back to the stands. Rob was already down at the front with his mates. He had dished the beers out and made no effort to watch for our return. I just hoped he was holding the right drink. His voice echoed in my mind: "I swear to God if you mess in my business again..." And suddenly all of my confidence was replaced by an aching feeling of impending doom.

There was only one race left. We had maybe twenty minutes for the drug to take effect.

"What was it?" Carys asked Kelly when we were

comfortably back in our spot. "What did you put in his drink?"

"GHB," shouted Kelly over the rowdy crowd, and then, because Carys was still looking confused, she added, "date rape drug."

"How do you have date rape drug?" asked Erin, looking shocked and possibly slightly impressed.

Kelly shrugged. "I just know someone that can get it."

"How will we know when it takes effect?" I said, staring at the back of Rob's head. He was wearing his top hat again.

"It's just like they're really drunk, so he might stumble or look like he's about to fall asleep. Or he might actually fall asleep. When that happens, one of us needs to make a move," said Kelly.

"I'll do it," said Carys, with surprising confidence. "I doubt that he's mentioned you or any of us to his friends or his brother, but just in case he has, they are least likely to suspect me. I just blend into the background."

This was simply not true. Carys was definitely not a blend-into-the-background type. In fact, I'd seen several men, and women, checking her out all afternoon. She was probably just one of those really annoying drop-dead-gorgeous-but-doesn't-know-it types. To be honest I didn't think they actually existed.

Part of me wanted to do it. Be the one to make the move and capture Rob. Make up for my mistake earlier. How could I have ballsed it up so badly that he didn't even give me time to explain? But I found myself nodding along to Carys' suggestion. I really didn't want to fail again. Plus, there was always the chance he could still recognise me – even off his tits on the drug – and kick off.

"I swear there's been half an hour between all the other races but this one is about five hours," said Erin. She kept trying to make eye contact with me, and was nervously passing her phone between her hands. I was pretty sure she wanted to call the police.

I pretended I didn't notice and focused all my attention on Rob, waiting for any miniscule change in his behaviour. He *did* seem to be getting floppier; his elbow kept slipping off the white railing that he was leaning on, and his head looked like it was drawing small circles in the air.

The final race was about to begin. The familiar preparatory hush was instilling among the crowd. The wave was ebbing again. Everyone's heads were turned to the right, staring at the blurry white shape that was the starting block. Everyone except Rob, who was now folded double on top of the railing, his head laid on the white metal and his arms hanging limply over the other side.

Kelly jabbed me hard in the ribs with her elbow. "I think he's aslee—"

But the rest of her sentence was drowned out by the unimaginable resonance of the final wave crashing onto the shore.

As the horses drew level with the stands, their hooves carving their beat into my chest, and the final crescendo was reached, Rob's head slid off the railing, his whole body swung under the barrier and collapsed in a heap on the grass.

That was it, the last race. People began unceremoniously filing out of the grounds. A few small clusters of people hung around to continue drinking or chatting, and some people went off to collect their final winnings. Rob's friends barely seemed to notice that he had passed out face down on the ground. I glanced around; there were a fair few other people sleeping off the effects of the race day.

"Come on mate," said one of the men he was with. They were laughing. They tried to pull him back under the railings, banging his head on the white metal of the pole as they did. One of his friends fell to his backside, laughing. The man with the same shape shoulders heaved him back into a standing position. Rob was awake and smiling – he leaned heavily on the barrier.

I exchanged nervous glances with the other moms. What should we do? Perhaps Bradley was just going to pop Rob in the car and take him home, then we would have missed our chance altogether.

"Alright, mate, see you later," Rob said to one, or two of the men, and lifted his hand lazily.

Bradley slapped him on the back, and said "If you're sure mate?"

"Yeah, yeah, she's driving." He stumbled forward again, clutching the railing for support.

Bradley bent down, picked up Rob's abandoned top hat and pushed it, lopsidedly, back onto his brother's head. "See you tomorrow then." And he and the other men from the party walked away, leaving Rob swaying on the spot, alone once more.

"Now. Go now!" I said, with a small push on Carys' back.

We ran to the end of the aisle, Carys leading the pack, and bolted down the steps.

We had just reached the bottom-most level, when a short blonde woman wearing a sequined white cami top and peach-coloured circle skirt appeared from nowhere, hooked her arm around Rob's back, her other under his armpit, and began to lead him towards the exit. She threw her hair over her shoulder, momentarily making eye contact with me.

It was Ella Ritchie, Rob's fiancée.

Also, the woman we'd hit on the head with a cork.

CHAPTER SIX

That was it then. We had lost him.

Ella aided him through the grounds, heading for the exit. There was no way we would catch them in time, and even if we did what would I say? *"Excuse me but can we kidnap your fiancée?"*

Fuck it. It was just one fail after another.

We should have just called the police at the start of the races, at least then we would have known he would've been there the whole time. What was I thinking? I wanted to be the one to deliver him to the police, and prove to myself and everyone else I could take care of things. I wanted to be the hero.

"Shit," said Carys, as we all stood there and watched Ella lead Rob out of sight.

We could do nothing but shake our heads.

"Come on then," I sighed to the moms. We made our way back down the stands and out through the tunnel to the car park.

"I'm sorry hun, I thought it was going to work," said

Erin, putting her arm around me. This time she was avoiding eye-contact.

"Me too," said Carys.

"It was a great plan," said Kelly.

No it wasn't, it was a shit plan, in retrospect. Kelly was merely humouring me. I wondered if any of them actually thought that it would work – or had they just come for a nice day at the races?

"What should we do now?" I said. I wanted to be annoyed at the others for not coming up with a better plan, and for letting me ruin the rubbish one that I had, but I could only blame myself.

We emerged at the other end of the tunnel and began looking for our cars, which was easier than I imagined, as the car park was getting fairly empty.

"Kelly, how did you get here? Do you need a lift ba—"

"Hello, um, excuse me," said a soft voice from behind.

I whirled around at the sound. The voice belonged to the blonde-haired Ella. Rob was slumped against a red brick wall adjacent to the tunnel; it looked like he might be asleep.

"Hi sorry, um, this is going to be weird, but I overheard you in the bar. Are you friends with Marie?"

"Yes we are," I said. I scrutinised her face. She was in her early twenties, I would say, and she was wearing a very thick layer of foundation.

"I've never met her. I know about her." Her tone was light and conversational, but there was something going unsaid, like when you know a 'but' is coming. "I just wondered why you wanted to speak to Rob?"

"What do you mean?" asked Erin, in her kindly American voice.

"You said 'can we just talk please?' I was wondering what you wanted to speak to him about? Is it Marie?"

I thought that it was probably best to tell the truth; there was something earnest about Ella, something vulnerable. "Yes. He beat her and put her in hospital." She was nodding as though this wasn't new information. "There's a warrant out for his arrest," I continued, "and we were hoping to get him to hand himself in."

Ella snorted. "Sorry, I didn't mean to laugh. It's just... he would never do that. He's done nothing wrong – in his mind – she provokes him. Literally every single time this happens, he comes running to me to lay low for a while until she's fine with it again. She'll never press charges. Do you know that? No matter what he's done to her, she always takes him back."

"Why are you two engaged then, if he's like that? Why don't you leave him?" said Kelly.

"I... He's still married to Marie. They'd have to get a divorce first and I know he'd never let that happen. It's just... He's a very difficult man to say no to. He makes it so that you don't have a choice." She rubbed her sandals against the gravel.

About ten seconds went by without anybody talking. Ella looked down at her feet, massaging her tummy gently, and then over at Rob. He was still out for the count. Carys was biting her thumb nail again.

"Did you drug him?" Ella asked looking at me.

"Uh..."

"I did," said Kelly, indifferently. "We were going to drag him to the police station if he didn't agree to go on his own."

Ella watched Rob for a few more seconds.

"You know, I want to leave him. I think about it all the time. I don't have a car though. I can't do it on my own."

Her focus was still on Rob, so it gave us time to wordlessly communicate to one another. What did she mean, *I don't have a car?* And then it hit me.

"Do you want us to take him to the police station?" I said, watching carefully for Ella's reaction.

She turned her tear-tracked face back into the sunlight and towards us. "Convincing Rob to hand himself in was never going to work but, maybe, you could try convincing Marie to press charges? That would do more for your cause." And then she smiled. It was a fleeting, one-sided smile, and she walked away, leaving Rob snoring against the wall.

"Right let's get this bastard in your car, Jaime," said Kelly, stomping in her heels over to him.

"I'll bring the car around," I called to the other three, and dashed off.

Not daring to think about what was happening in case thinking about it made it stop happening, I pelted across the car park. Half-running, half-bunny hopping, because it's physically impossible to run in heels on gravel, I got to the car, jumped in, and drove it through the gaps in the car park where other cars had already left. I felt like a rally driver. I didn't bother to take my heels off or even do my seat belt up – consequently the car was now bing-bonging manically at me. But it didn't matter, it was finally going to plan… sort of. Maybe I could do a really cool handbrake turn in front of the other moms, if only I actually knew how to do one.

When I pulled up by the tunnel entrance, Rob was standing with the aid of Kelly, Carys, and Erin, and was smiling, albeit a slightly dazed smile. I jumped out of the driver's seat to help them load him into the back.

"Oh my god, I know you," he said, grinning and swaying from side to side. He lunged forward, possibly to hug me. I couldn't be sure what his intentions were, so I skipped to the side out of his way. He fell onto his knees, in front of the car, smacking his head on the driver's side door frame. "FUCK!" he screamed rubbing his forehead.

"Get him in the car," yelled Erin, opening the back door.

The few people that remained in the race grounds were beginning to stare.

Kelly reached around and put her hand across his shoulder, and with startling strength she heaved him into the back seat, making sure to bash his head on the door frame once more on the way in. She whipped the belt around him, clipped it in, and slammed the door shut. It was an impressive backseat buckling manoeuvre and pretty obvious that she had older kids.

"It was so lovely to meet you all finally," she said through heavy breathing to Carys and Erin, and gave them both quick hugs. "We'd better go," she said to me, and then ran around the car and jumped in the passenger seat.

That was my cue to go, and quickly. "I'll message you both later, thanks for all your help today." I hugged them. "I can't believe we did it!"

Carys and Erin waved us off from the side of the car park. Rob stared out of the window and happily waved back.

"Where are we going?" he said as I drove over a cattle grate, making the car vibrate. "Uhuhuhuhuhuhuh," he laughed, like a toddler. And then he fell asleep.

"Thank God," I said, looking in my rear view mirror.

"What a fucking moron," said Kelly, looking at Rob like he was a poo on my backseat. She turned to me. "Do you know where the station is?"

"It's in my sat nav already."

"Ooh prepared, I like it." She brought up the sav nav

function on the car's dashboard computer, and clicked 'start journey'.

The station was seven minutes drive away.

"Well, I had a lovely day today," she said. "Shame I didn't win anything, but I only put one bet on."

"Oh yeah, I meant to ask earlier, what does each way mean?" I was trying to keep one eye on the road ahead and one on the sleeping Rob in my mirror.

"Hmm? Oh, it just splits your bet, so that half of your money is betting that the horse will win and half is betting that it will place, either first or second or third, whatever. So, if the horse wins, you win twice, but say it only comes second then you still win, but just not as much."

"Oh right." Still didn't understand.

"What will happen to him now?" said Kelly, jerking her head to the side. "Will he go to prison?"

"Honestly, I'm not too sure. I hope so. I mean, you would think so right? I guess we'll have to convince Marie to press charges like Ella told us. I'll ask my friend Niamh to speak to her, she's a family lawyer, and she's really, really, good."

Niamh. My only real friend. I'd been neglecting our relationship. I had been so caught up in plotting to catch Rob, and planning my route to promotion, that I had completely forgotten to check in on her. She said something about an interview... Or did I completely make that up? I should buy her a present, and a card, in case she won the Lawyer of the Year tonight – that would go some way to atone for my guilt.

"How's Rosie?" I said, realising I had been silent for a few moments.

"Yeah really good, she's very nearly walking. She's taken a few steps."

"Wow, that's early. River only just learned to crawl last month."

"I keep trying to video it on my phone, but it's so difficult. My first was walking at nine months too."

There was a groan from the backseat. Rob lifted his head, and then let it drop back down again. It thudded as it hit the window.

"Bloody hell, I thought he was going to wake up then," laughed Kelly.

"Where are we going?" came his low, drawling slurs.

"Good morning, sleepyhead," said Kelly brightly, turning around to face him.

"Who are you?" he said, an edge returning to his voice.

Kelly turned to me and whispered, "I've got more if we need to give him some."

Two minutes to the station.

"I'm hungry," he said. "Are you the taxi driver?"

"Yes I am," I said, glancing in the mirror. There were shadows emerging on his face where the various parts of my car had kissed him.

"Thanks. You can let me out here." He unbuckled his seat belt, grabbed the handle, and with a mighty heave he threw all his weight at the door. It stayed firmly shut, and he rebounded into a heap in the footwell.

"Child lock," I said.

"I'm hungry, let me out." He pushed himself back into the seat and repeatedly grabbed at the handle again.

Thirty seconds to the station.

"We're just going to get a kebab; do you want one?" said Kelly.

We pulled into the station car park. Rob stared blankly out of the window at the red brick building, his eyes raking over the black and white station signage and the parked police vehicles out the front.

"Hey! This isn't Abra-kebab-ra!" he cried.

I jumped out of the car and opened Rob's door.

"Come on then, out we come," I said, with the air of encouraging a cat to go outside.

Rob climbed out of the car like a two-year-old walking down stairs, very gingerly, in reverse and on his knees. I grabbed the manila file that I had prepared the previous Friday. It was in the pocket behind my seat, in front of Rob the whole time, and pushed it into Rob's chest. He took possession of it without question.

I took his left arm, Kelly his right, and we walked into the station as a threesome.

The officer behind the desk was young, bald, and his shirt was perfectly pressed. He looked each of us up and down in turn, and said, "Can I help?"

I stepped forward. "My friend is very drunk, but he wishes to hand himself in."

"Hand himself in for...?"

"Go on, give him your file," I encouraged Rob.

He looked at me, frowning, looked down at the big beige envelope and pushed it, with great concentration – his tongue poking out the corner of his mouth – through the gap between the counter and the glass. The police officer opened it and briefly looked through the contents. It included copies of every shred of evidence that I could collate on his crime; photos of Marie's battered face, and a print out of the actual 'wanted gallery' from the Westmidland's police website.

Bald Guy held up a picture of Rob's face. "Is this you? Robert Sparks?"

Rob laughed and pointed at the picture. "Yeah." Then

he looked at me as if I was supposed to see something funny in it, like a bad hairstyle.

"Have you been drinking, Rob?" said the officer.

"Duh," said Rob, stumbling a few feet forward, his hand slipping off the counter edge.

The officer jammed his hand against something we couldn't see on his side of the desk. Within seconds there was a hiss, and the door next to the counter swung open. Two police officers, one male and one female, and the bald counter guy, raced out.

"And you want to hand yourself in?" said Bald Guy. "For assaulting your wife?"

Rob clicked his tongue and rolled his eyes. "What's that bitch said now?" He said it in a casual, jokey kind of way, but nobody laughed.

"I'm going to arrest you now; do you understand what I'm doing?"

Rob rolled his eyes again and shook his head. "Urgh, fucking get on with it then!" He held out his arms, wrists pointing upwards.

With the tiniest glance towards the other officers, Bald Guy took his handcuffs from his belt and snapped them over Rob's wrists.

I permitted myself a second's glance at Kelly, who was stood hands on hips, beaming and nodding along to the officer's talk.

"Robert Sparks, I'm arresting you on suspicion of assault. You do not have to say anything, but it may harm your defence if you do not mention, when questioned, something you later rely on in court. Anything you do say may be given in evidence. Do you understand?"

Rob swayed on his feet lurching to the left and crashing into the woman police officer.

The officers helped straighten him up again.

"Do you understand?" Bald Guy repeated.

"I... really need a piss!" said Rob.

The officers shared quick looks. Then Bald Guy said, "We're going to take a breath test. Do you consent?"

Rob raised his shoulders. This meant 'whatever.'

"Are you also under the influence of any drugs?"

Oh shit.

I side-eye looked at Kelly. If they suspected he was taking drugs they might take a blood test. A blood test would show up GHB in his system. Kelly was resolutely not looking at me, but her eyes were wide and staring at Rob, waiting for his response.

"Fuck off am I," he shouted.

"You can just say no, you don't have to swear at us," said the woman police officer. She looked at Kelly and me. "Has he been driving?"

"NO!" both Kelly and I said in unison.

Bald Guy and the woman officer then push-walked Rob through the door leading behind the counter.

The other male officer looked at me.

"My contact details are in that file," I told him.

He looked at the watch on his wrist and the clock on the wall (surely they said the same thing) and shook his head. "Then we will call you if we need any more info," he said, and then followed the others through the door. He closed it, picked up the papers on top on the envelope, and flicked his eyes towards the door: a dismissal.

My heart skipped a beat. It was finally all over. We raced out of the station and back into my car. It felt like only moments ago we'd been in the marquee bar trying to convince an irate wife beater to 'have a chat'.

We burst out laughing the moment we sat down.

"We did it!" I cried.

"Fucking yes!" screamed Kelly, and high-fived me.

"Quick tell Marie," I said, pulling down my seat belt.

"Already on it." Kelly pulled her phone out of her bra.

I caught a flash of the ForumFriends home page on the screen.

"Where do you want me to drop you off? I have this work thing tonight so I'm not sure I can take you back to Derby."

"Oh that's OK, can you drop me at the coach station? It's just around the corner. Look, Marie's replied. Ah…she just said 'hmmmm'. What does that even mean? Isn't she happy?"

"I'm not sure," I said, glimpsing the phone. "I guess it's not that straightforward. They were together since college weren't they? He's all she's known."

We were silent for a few moments.

"Well, I hope he goes down long enough for her to realise she's better without him." She let out a long puff and stuffed her phone back in her bra.

"Hopefully."

Right, so now I just needed to persuade Marie to press charges so that Rob actually serves time, something she's never done before. At least I can use my awesome lawyer skills that failed me earlier…

The drive back to Birmingham was relatively traffic-free, though there wouldn't be enough time to go home, freshen up and drive back before I had to be at the CRAPs at six.

But I was *starving*, I had a thumping headache – probably from not drinking enough all day – and my rock-hard breasts were not only leaking through my pads but threatening to burst from my £400 Rueberry original gown. I would stop at Tesco on the way and get some supplies.

It was 5 p.m. Oliver would be picking River up from nursery right now.

Oh no! FOMO!

I miss her so much.

Her adorable little face – I just want to eat it – and her laugh, oh my, that laugh. I want to rub her face on my face, and blow raspberries on the soles of her feet.

Great, now I'm crying.

Oh no, and cramps! Better get some tampons too, just in case.

I drove into Tesco car park and autopiloted over to the parent and child spaces before remembering I was alone, so I pulled into the nearest empty spot. Good job anyway because the bastard BMW wankers were back in their favourite space, and I didn't really fancy another scene. I was far too delicate and hormonal; too close to the edge.

I climbed out of the car, popped my shoes back on, and went through my shopping list in my head: water, sandwiches, a card and maybe some chocolates for Niamh, tampons, paracetamol...

Another mom was walking towards me from the store. She was carrying a baby on her left hip, and in her right hand she held shopping bags and a lead with a backpack-wearing toddler on the end. She had reached the point where the BMW was parked, when one of the carrier bags in her hands burst open, spilling its entire contents onto the asphalt.

"Oh, for God's sake," she muttered, bending down.

A carton of milk had splatted to the ground like a giant seagull shit, and apples and oranges were now rolling under the BMW and into the road. Her toddler, upon seeing a packet of Blue Ribands torn from the bag, began screaming his head off, which in turn set the baby crying. My breasts pulsated at the noise.

Instinctively I rushed over and began scooping up fruit from the road, which was fucking difficult in this dress.

"What in the hell is going on?" It was that bloody moustachioed BMW prick. "I can see you from the cafe." He said flapping his arms towards the store windows and back at the car. He stepped right over the mom, her groceries, her toddler, and me, and began buffing the side of the car with his jacket sleeve. He licked his thumb and began rubbing at an invisible spot, his face inches away from the bodywork.

"The bag wasn't anywhere near your precious car," I shouted over the crying children.

"Lucky for you then," he hissed. He cast his eyes over the scattered groceries, shook his head, and stepped right back over us, headed straight back for the shop.

"Not going to help?" I called after him, but he completely ignored me and walked back into the store.

"Typical," said the mom, barely audible over the wailing. She grabbed the Blue Ribands and deftly unwrapped one with one hand, shoving it into the toddler's mouth, he stopped crying.

"What's the difference between BMWs and hedgehogs?" I said.

She looked at me and shrugged.

"Hedgehogs have pricks on the outside."

"HA!"

"I got that one from the Internet – you can keep it. I've had run ins with that guy before," I said, thinking back to the beans aisle.

"Urgh, so have I. He's a right See You Next Tuesday. I wish I had scratched his car, actually."

"Where are you parked? I've got extra carrier bags in my boot."

The mom stood up and pointed to her car, it was the one directly behind mine. "That's my car, the red one."

Balancing all the fruit that I could rescue, the mom and I walked over to our cars. I waved my foot under the rear bumper and the boot hissed and popped open. Inside, I always keep a carrier bag stuffed with other carrier bags, and laying on top on my bag of bags, which I had totally forgotten about, were Clive's one of a kind, custom-made, £4000, golf clubs.

I bit my lip and glanced back at the BMW. A surge of adrenaline pulsed through my chest, and down into my fingertips. Why did I feel so dangerous? Was it the hormones? Or perhaps the infallible feeling of finally delivering Rob to the police?

I saw Rob's crooked little smile swim before my eyes. I thought I'd be pleased that we finally had him, but I felt… angry, like a fire was growing in my chest. I closed my eyes, and tried to steady my rapid breathing and heart rate, but Clive was there, and Ryan too, and Carol from the library, and the BMW wankers, and all the people in the supermarket who jumped out of my way and avoided me instead of offering help; like I was some noisy infectious disease. The fire was spreading, clawing up my chest.

No!

A panic, a darkness. The flames were threatening to burst from my mouth, to run out down my arms and fingers.

I reached out and took the closest club from its box. I barely even realised I was doing it.

I glanced over at Mr BMW, who was sitting in the café again. I'm not sure that I even saw him, maybe I completely imagined him there. My vision felt kind of… hazy. And my ears were filled with a high-pitched screeching; it drowned out everything. It was like in the movies when a bomb goes off and afterwards all you can hear is a sonorous peal to let you know that the main character has gone temporarily deaf, or is in shock. That was me; in shock.

In hindsight I would say I only wanted to scratch it a little, teach him a lesson – that there are many more important things in this world to worry about than shiny cars – and that just a little ding would do the trick, but the reality is that I was no longer in control of my own actions, or emotions.

I came to a stop level with the backdoor on the driver's side, and planted my heels into the asphalt, about a foot apart.

Just a little scratch.

I thought back to last week: he let me walk in the pissing rain with my baby – my tiny baby! – and we were soaked… He didn't give a fuck.

I raised the club above my head with both hands, paused for a fraction of a second, and in a firm arc, brought the thing down onto the bastarding wing mirror. Metal connected to plastic and both were catapulted to the ground with an exquisite smash. The mirror glass exploded at my feet, and bare wires hung from the hole where the mirror once was.

With a mere moment's pause, I walked to the boot of the car. I should have stopped there.

An associate that brings coffee…

"AGHHHHHHHH!"

I swung the club out to the side and back into the car, straight through the clear red and orange plastic of the driver's side rear lights.

The mom who was still standing at my open boot, dropped all the recently retrieved fruits, her mouth falling open like a cartoon character.

People were beginning to gather.

And still I did not stop.

At least you'll actually be working, and not just fannying about on reception with your knickers on show...

"FUCK YOU, CLIVE!"

Smash!

The passenger side rear lights were now lying in colourful shards on the asphalt.

I was at the front of the car. I wiggled my dress up over my knees, and climbed on top of the bonnet. The hood clunked under the heels of my shoes with that weird noise metal makes when it bends, and, making sure that I was properly balanced, I swung the club – hard – onto the windscreen.

SMACK!

A pea-sized dent appeared in the centre of the glass.

SMACK!

Now it looked like a bullet hole.

SMACK!

A sound like the starting pistol at the racecourse rang through the car park, and the windshield burst into a hundred million pieces. A violent orgasm of broken glass.

The world slowly clawed its way back into focus. I was on top of a bonnet. Glass everywhere. The ringing faded, and I was aware of people shouting, gasping, laughing.

People were filming me with their phones. Standing only metres away. Nobody spoke to me, nobody said anything – they just pointed their screens and gawped.

What did I just do?

I lobbed the perfectly unscathed club inside the – now exposed – BMW interior and climbed down from the hood, avoiding the bulk of the shards.

"My CAAAAAAAAARRRRRRRRRR!" came a

loud, guttural scream. BMW guy was running, *running*, towards the now-glittering wreck.

Holy fuck, what did I just do?

I walked straight past him and into the store. I didn't look at him. He barely noticed me. He could have punched me right then in the face and I would have probably accepted that I deserved it. The fire that was burning in my chest was now threatening to make its way out as vomit, and with every thud of my accelerating heartbeat, the vomit grew closer to my mouth.

Inside the store, I expected that somebody might challenge me; an innocent bystander shopper? The manager? Security? BMW guy himself? But people just stared open-mouthed at me. No, wait – they were actively avoiding me, grabbing their kids and shopping and running out of the store. That makes the second time in two weeks.

I picked up a bottle of water from the fridge by the entrance and grabbed the first 'congratulations' card that I could see. The sandwiches and paracetamol would have to wait; they were too far back in the store.

I slapped a tenner onto the cigarettes checkout counter – fuck the change – and speed-walked out of the store. The mom that I tried to help earlier was gone already; legged it, probably didn't want to be associated with me. Can't say I blame her.

Halfway to the car I pulled off my heels and began to run. I was now made entirely of adrenaline. There was still fruit everywhere. I got in the driver's seat, just as two burly security types came pelting out of the entrance.

Wow they run fast.

I slammed the car into reverse, the boot still standing erect, and sped backwards out of the space, abruptly stopping short of smashing into the car parked opposite. I whacked it back into first, second, third, and sped off through the car park. I was faintly aware of a rolling tumbling noise coming from my boot area. I think that must have been the other club leaving my car. And possibly my carrier bag of bags. Fuck, there was at least five quid's worth of bags in there.

I reached the exit to Tesco car park, and the two security guys – who now stopped chasing me – stood with their hands on their hips. Actually, I think one of them was using his radio. He was probably calling the police right now.

Fuckity fuck! I am in serious trouble.

I drove as quickly as I could for as long as I dared. Would they follow me? Would the police come straight away? Why did I do it?

I forgot the fucking tampons.

Fuck! Fuck! Fuck!

Eventually, after circling the area a few times, I pulled into a layby near the CRAPs venue and necked the bottle of water. It was far enough away that I could hide here in the car, but close enough that I could see the entrance. The party would be starting any minute now. Lauren would be expecting me to meet her in the lobby so that she could run through, for the eightieth time, her militant schedule. My head was still pounding, my tits were leaking boulders, and now I was probably bleeding through my sequins. I closed my eyes and waited for the police to find me. Maybe I should let Oliver know that I won't be home tonight. It's such a shame that I wouldn't get to deliver my speech.

There was a rapping on the window. I was surely busted. I flung my eyes open – it was dark now. My heart smashed against my ribcage; how long had I been asleep?

Niamh banged on the window again and pulled the car door open.

"What are you doing out here? It's eight o clock! Lauren's going spare," she laughed. "Did you know your boot is open?"

"Fuck! I thought you were the police!"

"What?!"

I stood up, steadying myself on the door. I looked up and down the street – no sign of the police yet. I wondered if they were waiting for me at home; sitting in the living room with Olly having a nice cup of tea, eating my custard creams.

"You look…" Niamh began, eyeing me up and down.

Nice? Terrible? Both would have been accurate.

"Come on, let's get inside." She wrapped her arm around my back and aided me in the direction of the hotel. "Have you been drinking?"

The bright lights in the hotel lobby had a sobering effect and, by the time we walked into the darkened party hall, I felt much more rebalanced. My tits were still engorged, and a dull ache emanated from my abdomen.

"Oh shit, Niamh, am I bleeding? I think I came on."

Niamh leaned behind me and looked at my ass.

"No hun, you're not bleeding. Are you okay though? Like, mentally?"

I wasn't sure how to answer that question, so I gave her a 'we'll talk about it later' look. She nodded and squeezed my arm. That's why I loved her; I didn't even need to explain anything, she just knew.

The party in the main hall was already in full swing. There was a disco, and a dozen or so tables draped in white cloths along the perimeter of the dance floor. People from all the branches were there in their glittery party clothes. It reminded me of the Christmas do, but with slightly less debauchery. Deciding on the spot that I would get a taxi home – so long as I wasn't arrested before then – I snatched two glasses of Cava from the welcome drinks table and handed one to Niamh.

"Not long now 'til your big speech. You nervous?" Niamh said, taking a sip.

"No," I said truthfully. "Not after the day I've had." I threw back my Cava and grabbed another.

"Jaime, I must say… your speech…" Frances appeared from nowhere and cut into the gap between Niamh and me. "It moved me." She patted her chest theatrically. "You deliver that speech tonight, and that job is as good as yours."

"Thank you," I said, not really sure what I should believe at the moment.

"Don't thank me, you're a very clever woman." She gave me a little pat on the arm. "You've got this." She sauntered off into the dark of the room holding her drink.

I turned to Niamh but we were cut apart again, this time by Clive. The flames in my chest whirred again.

"G'evening Jaime, Niamh." His already-unfocused eyes were now looking in completely opposite directions, and he was slightly wobbly on his feet.

"He's pissed," Niamh mouthed behind him.

"Hello, Clive, having a good evening?" I said, barely pretending that I cared.

Clive grunted. Presumably this meant yes. "Did you get my golf clubs?" he slurred, swinging one of his eyes in my direction.

"Yeah, uh…they're in the car."

He grunted again.

"I would've gotten them myself, but Ryan and I have been working on securing a few more of the Montgomery family. Did you know they're related to Fergie?" He laughed.

The honest answer was no, but if I were to say no, I would be risking a boring and lengthy story about the lineage of some clients that, in Clive's eyes, made them better people, and most probably he would find some way to work in his tale about how he once, in the nineties, beat Prince Andrew in a thrilling round of golf. Everyone at work knew this story by heart now, but of course nobody believed it had actually happened. I gave a noncommittal shrug-nod that could have passed as a yes.

"Have you spoken to IT yet?" I said, trying to change the subject as quickly as possible.

"I'm sorry, what d'you mean?" said Clive, his other eye whizzing around to focus on me.

"You said that you could sort something out with IT about the problems HR are having with their computers. If I got your clubs. Remember?"

"Sorry, you've totally lost me." He looked from me to Niamh, his crooked mouth hanging open, showing off his yellowing bottom teeth.

"But you said—" I began.

"Jaime, he's lying. There is no IT problem in HR. I spoke to Celia today, they said they sent your training schedule to Clive last week," said Niamh, shaking her head. "Is that what he told you? Fuck's sake Clive, why are you lying?"

Clive was blinking rapidly, looking from Niamh to me, to Niamh again, probably wishing he hadn't had so much to drink and therefore could untangle his story with a clear head. "I... Uh..."

I rounded on him. "You mean to tell me I've been shadowing that oaf all this time, when I could have been back up to speed by now? Explain it."

Niamh squared her shoulders and closed in on him.

"Well... now... uh, you mustn't take this the wrong way," he stammered, "it's just that... in my experience... that is... with you women going off and having babies... well, is it really worth putting you through the training if you're just going to go off on maternity leave again and have to do it all over yet another time? I mean... financially... it doesn't make sense for the company to pay for you to do the same training repeatedly."

WTF!

Niamh's eyes were wide, and she was staring at me, not Clive. This was her 'I'm about to kick off' face.

"What the fu—" she began, but I held up my hand to stop her.

"OK, let me get this straight," I said to Clive, "the only reason you haven't put me through the training is because *you* think it's pointless and a waste of money because I'll definitely be going off and having more babies?"

"In my experience, women don't have just the one baby. Not when it's a choice between staying at home or doing actual work."

"Oh my god." I put my fingers to my temples. I needed a few moments to process this bullshit.

Niamh looked ready to punch his lights out.

"So, you're saying you never had any intention of sorting out my training? You were just going to fob me off until I went off on maternity leave again?"

Clive replicated my shrug-nod.

"Unbelievable!" I said. "You know, I'm pretty sure that's illegal."

"It most definitely *is* illegal," interjected Niamh.

Clive shrugged; he didn't even look remotely abashed. "Sorry darlin', I'm not the only partner that thinks this way. What can you do about it?"

"Not Frances," said Niamh, "she put forward Jaime for the partner position."

"Frances has always been the exception to the rule – why do you think she's leaving? And trying to shoehorn in another bloody snowflake before she goes; sneaky. It'll never work though." He closed his eyes and shook his head. "Not here."

"Well, we'll take it to tribunal then," said Niamh. They were literally chest to chest.

"Wait!" I downed my second glass of bubbly, reached across to the table, picked up a third and necked that too. "I've got a better idea."

CHAPTER SEVEN

"Places everyone, places. We're about to announce the Lawyer of the Year award," said Lauren to the room at large. She rushed over to me. "You ready? Do you remember the plan?" Her face was sweaty, her fancy up-do had already started to tumble out over her shoulders, and she kept rubbing her palms onto her – thankfully – black, party dress.

"Yes. You've told me about eight times already—"

She ploughed on at breakneck speed anyway. "OK, so, you just walk onto the stage from the side, don't trip, stand behind the podium and speak into the microphone, not too far away because we won't hear you, but not too close because it'll get feedback, which is annoying for everyone. Make sure you thank all the partners and acknowledge all the nominees – there's a list waiting for you on the podium – deliver your speech. It's really good, Fran told me all about it, well done, I can't wait. Then announce the winner. Don't do that really annoying thing and pause for ages before you say who it is, OK? But don't rush it either. When the winner comes up on stage to receive their award, make sure they give a speech, and if they don't seem like they will, then push them for one, but don't let it go on too long. That's it. Simple, huh?" She exhaled hard and put her hand on her chest.

"Are you OK, Lauren? You look like you might be sick."

She swallowed and waved her hand in front of her mouth. "I'm fine. Are you ready?" She looked over at one of the other admin guys, who was standing at the side of the stage giving a thumbs up.

I took one last look at Clive. Apart from his moustache slightly twitching, his face was impassive again. He had no idea what was about to hit him. "Absolutely," I said, and Lauren placed her hands on the small of my back and threw me towards the stage.

I climbed up the steps onto the platform. There was a whiteboard, onto which they had projected a dancing clipart logo of the word CRAP. Next to the this was the podium, a cheap, white, MDF plinth with a shiny table top, not too dissimilar to Clive's compromised desk. I stood behind it and gazed out into the dark hall space, trying to make out faces, but the spotlight was shining straight into my eyes. All I could see was a sea of blank white blobs, and occasional brown ones, among the glittery, floating dust. I fought against my eyes doing that tunnel vision thing again.

Niamh stood in the centre of the dance floor alone, one hand on her hip, the other holding her cava at thigh level. I squinted at her; she was wearing an expression that I recognised immediately to be her 'this'll be good' look.

I tapped the mic and the beat reverberated around the hall. It felt like each time I spotted a person and turned my eyes to them, they would vanish into the darkness. I clocked most of the partners and some of the other nominees dotted about, though I only really knew them from photos on their online work profiles. And then I saw Ryan, in his best hipster shirt and knob-head dickie bow, sitting at the closest table. It would be the shortest walk to the stage if he won. Did he already know something?

Clive was now a mere lurking shadow at the back of the hall, his arms folded over his chest. It was impossible to see where either of his eyes were pointed.

I leaned forward into the microphone. "Hello, everyone," I whispered.

"Louder!" yelled Ryan. "We can't hear you!" He and a few people from his table guffawed.

"How's this?" I shouted, clenching my jaw. A screeching feedback noise rang around the hall – most people screwed up their faces against it.

I sighed, wiped my brow, and carried on. "Thank you all for coming to the CRAPs tonight. What an amazing event Lauren and..." – fuck, I'd forgotten the rest of the admins' names. I think one may have been Andy? – "...the admin team have laid on. Let's all give them a round of applause, shall we?"

There was a small trickle of muted clapping. Lauren smiled and waved, but quickly stopped at the lacklustre response.

I surveyed the crowd, my eyes beginning to adjust to the darkness. Some of the party-goers were on their phones, probably texting, or scrolling through endless shit on ForumFriends.

I remembered how humble and appreciative the admins had been when I'd made them coffee, and how they'd welcomed me into their office when I needed a place to express. These phone twats don't care about the admins. Maybe I was no better, I can't even remember their names. Dan, maybe? I think the tall one is Dan. I tried to smile at Lauren and the other guys, but my face seemed to have spasmed into a permanent grimace. My heart was drumming hard in my chest, threatening to burst through my – now probably unsalvageable – dress.

"Lauren and her team have been working tirelessly over the past few weeks to make sure everything is perfect. And that is why, first and foremost, I need to apologise to them for what I am about to do. Lauren, Lauren's team, I'm so sorry.

Lauren stood frozen on the spot, her mouth opened slightly, her eyebrows knitting together in the middle of her forehead.

"Now, you are all expecting me to deliver a speech about Caine Reynolds and what an undying joy it is to work here, how amazing all of the people are, especially the partners, and what I wish for the future of this company, blah blah blah. And then I'm supposed to announce the Lawyer of the Year award."

The golden envelope and glass trophy sat expectantly on the podium.

"And for those of you who have read my speech already, you'll know what an absolute fucking blinder it was—"

"Hear hear!" said Niamh, laughing and raising her glass. People looked at her, but nobody joined in. Frances was rhythmically patting down her trousers and glancing between Niamh, Lauren, and I. Maybe she thought that we were plotting something together. Lauren looked on the very edge of crying, and/or vomiting.

"But I've had a change of heart," I said.

I heard these words float around the hall as crisp and confident as I had intended them to be. Nobody was on their phone anymore; everybody was watching me.

"I can't stand up here and say that this is a great place

to work, when, one," I held up a finger, "it's an antiquated, misogynistic, cesspool of buffoonery."

Ooh, nice words.

"And two," I held up a second finger, making a V sign and pointing it straight at Clive, "I no longer work here."

Everyone was rapt. White faces stared open-mouthed at me. Their silence was a solid presence.

"That's right, effective immediately, I quit. I quit this fucking place. I'm going to start my own practice with my Goode friend, Niamh. See what I did there? Goode, Niamh?"

A very quiet murmur erupted, and people squeezed closer to their neighbours. Nobody laughed.

"AND WHAT'S MORE," I shouted, silencing the room again, "I'm going to poach all your motherfucking clients, and there's nothing you can you about it, you mouldy old bunch of self-righteous, bigoted CUNTS!"

I looked at Niamh; she was grinning maniacally and holding her arm out at a weird angle. For a split second I thought she was doing a nazi salute, but then I realised she was trying to get me to do a mic drop.

"MIC DROP!" I screamed, and I threw the microphone like it was on fire onto the floor at front of the stage. It hit the carpet like a loud, thudding shit and rang a terrible cacophony of feedback throughout the hall. People's hands shot over their ears.

I snatched the golden envelope from the podium, leaving the piece of crap award where it was, and walked down the steps and off the stage.

"You're not supposed to say mic drop, you dick," said Ryan pedantically as I waltzed past.

"Fuck you, Ryan," I replied.

I walked across the dance floor, out of the hall, out of the hotel lobby, down the street, and sat in my car, waiting

– the third time that day – for the adrenaline to catch up with me.

Niamh got into the passenger seat. "That was brilliant," she laughed. "I can't believe you did that. *You*. Jaime Wright you fucking badass!"

I laughed. "Yeah, I am!"

"Is that the winner?" said Niamh, plucking the golden envelope out of my hands.

"Yeah, I suppose it is."

Niamh paused for a fraction of a second and then peeled back the flap of the envelope. She peered in and then quickly closed it again.

"Who won?" I asked.

"You don't want to know." She ripped the envelope in half and then in half again, and stuffed it in her bag.

That either meant it was her, and she didn't want me to know that I had denied her of her prize, or it was Ryan.

"I got you something," I said, fishing the greetings card from the passenger footwell. "Sorry, I haven't had a chance to write it out yet. It's a card to congratulate your win."

And to make up for being such a lousy friend recently.

"Thanks." Niamh took the card. "It says congratulations on passing your driving test."

"I was under a lot of time restraints," I added.

"So, we really going to do this? Start our own firm?"

I smiled. Guess there was no turning back now. Not after I'd told a room full of my contemporaries to go fuck themselves.

"I'm so excited Jaime. This has been my dream for years. Here, let's switch places, I'll drive you home."

I didn't have the heart to tell Niamh that I would probably have to serve a prison sentence before we got to start our own firm together. But that bit could wait.

"You're home early. I wasn't expecting you until much later." Oliver was on the sofa with an enormous plate of Chinese food in front of him, and sports or some shit on the telly. "Do you want some food?"

I collapsed onto the sofa next to him. "Yes please, I'm starving. I was going to get a sandwich, but the security guards were on my tail."

Oliver frowned and side-eyed me. "How were the CRAPs? And how was your moms' meet at the races? Hang on, let me get you some food, there's loads left over. I accidentally got a set meal for two."

Five minutes later, he came back into the living room bearing a mountain of noodles, ribs, spring rolls, and prawn crackers.

I told him all about my day, which seemed to have lasted approximately five years. I couldn't actually believe that it had all happened today. I told him how I picked up Clive's clubs from Naked Mole Rat Man; about how I met up with the moms, my emotionally-close but geographically-distant friends for the first time; how I went to the races, bet on a shit horse, drugged a wife-beating wanted criminal and dragged his ass to the police station; how I then went to Tesco for water and tampons and ended up losing my mind and smashing the fuck out of a man's car; and how I quit my job by calling all of my colleagues self-righteous, bigoted, cunts.

"And then I did a mic drop."

He blinked several times at me. I was half expecting to be reprimanded, to be called out for the stupid things I had done, and the stupid decisions I had made, but instead Oliver burst out laughing, winked at me and said, "You're a fugitive, that's fucking sexy."

I laughed. "OK, if you say so. Naimh and I are going to start our own firm."

"That sounds perfect, babe. Your own firm – you won't have to do wills and probate any more. So what are you going to do on Monday, then?"

I shrugged, "Just chill out for a bit I think and then I'll speak to Niamh and we can make some decisions about where we want our office to be and how we go about starting it all up. That is if I don't go to jail first."

He laughed. I couldn't tell if it was a genuine laugh, or a nervous one, or maybe both.

"How did River go down tonight?" I said.

"Yeah, alright, well… she shat in the bath – twice – and she wouldn't eat her sweet potato patties, or pasta… Phew, actually it was pretty hard. I don't know how you do it every day."

Later, in bed, I checked in on the moms' group. Immediately I was bombarded by thankful and congratulatory posts from all the moms, with the exception of Marie, who I had heard nothing but radio silence from. Eventually, when she starts speaking again, I will impress the importance of pressing charges, but for now it was nice just to feel like the hero. I updated them with the extra news of my work bombshell, heaved a great sigh, and fell back onto the mattress. I half-wondered if the police would arrive in the middle of the night, but I was asleep before my head hit the pillow.

Except they never did come, and as the weekend went on, I felt less and less sure that they would. Surely they had my details, my licence plate, my Clubcard number, or whatever. But nothing: no visit, no phone call, not even an email telling me what an awful criminal I was. And with the gradually decreasing threat of arrest, it turned out to be one of the best weekends ever. River let me lie in until 6:45 a.m. on Saturday and napped for a solid two hours during the day, so Oliver and I had sex in the afternoon, in the living room. Niamh WhatsApped me a few links she thought I might find helpful about starting our own practice; I skimmed through them but would have a better look on Monday. I just wanted to enjoy my weekend. The glorious weather from Friday continued right throughout; we went to the park, and pushed River on the swings for the first time, took twenty-thousand pictures, got tip-tops from the ice cream van, and then later we had orange chips and battered sausages in the car overlooking Lickey Hills. The sun streaming in through the windows made it feel like June, not March, and as a person whose mood is highly weather-dependant, I felt that nothing, even arrest, could bring me down now. My friends were safe, thanks to my actions – possibly Marie could even come out of hiding. And all because of me. I'd finally done something, finally stood up for myself and others. I was helpful. Maybe I could even win one of those 'Mum of the Year' awards you see in the local papers.

When I went to bed on Sunday night, the last thing I did was switch off the alarm for Monday morning. Oliver had promised me a genuine lie in. He would get River up and take her to nursery before he went to work so that I could wake up naturally for the first time in almost forever.

There was a distant drilling noise. It was getting louder and closer, whatever it was, and it was coming for me. Was it the dentist? It was penetrating right into my brain. If I could only see what it was.

It took an unholy effort to prise my eyes open. I lay there, staring at the source of the noise, my brain functioning a few seconds slower than my eyes. The alarm.

Urgh, I turned the alarm off.

I grabbed the phone and stared at the screen. Why, when it normally has a picture of a bell, did it have the words 'Clive Office' on it? It stopped buzzing. Good – shut up. I smacked it back down onto the pillow. It started again.

WTF is this? I sat up in bed and gawped down at it.

It wasn't an alarm at all – Clive was calling me.

Right now.

"Yeah?" I answered, my throat scratchy and dry.

"Where are you Jaime? It's half-past nine, we were supposed to have a meeting with Mrs. Montgomery at nine this morning."

"I don't work there anymore Clive. I quit, remember?"

"Yes, I certainly do remember that little scene you caused Jaime. But here's the thing you're forgetting: you still work here until you hand in your formal written resignation—"

"Fine I'll print one off and post it today."

"No, let me finish. I don't know if you remember the details of your contract, darlin' – it's rather a standard thing – but unless you want to repay all of your maternity leave back to us, you still have to work here for three months."

"What?"

"If you don't work your three months returning probationary, you have to pay back all of your maternity leave. Are you understanding me yet?"

I was on my feet. "What the...? That can't be true.

That's like..." I couldn't do the maths quickly enough: six months full-pay... About twenty-two thousand, plus three months half-pay or something... "That's like twenty-eight grand!"

"Actually it's closer to thirty, because of your annual leave days."

"I can't afford that."

"Exactly. So, you'll be here in twenty minutes. Twenty minutes, Jaime – you have a client meeting. And try to look decent this time."

"Fuck!"

I think I hung up the call. I threw the phone onto the bed. It bounced onto the floor.

"Fuck, fuck, FUCK!"

What was I going to do?

I leaned over the side of the bed, grabbed the phone, and punched Oliver's contact details up.

"Answer, please answer." Tears were streaming down my face.

"Hello, you are trying to reach me, Oliver. I am busy slogging for the man, call me later, or not at all, yeah? Don't leave a message." Beep.

"FUCK!" I screamed. I had to pick up River in a few hours. Do I go in? I can't go in. It would be hideous, just so embarrassing. Faces swam in front of my eyes: Clive, Ryan, Lauren. Bile was building at the back of my throat; it was getting really warm in this room.

I'd ask the other moms, on the group, what I should do – maybe one of them would have the answer? They had saved me so many times before, and I them. I wiped the tears from my face, and with trembling hands I opened the group on my phone. How would I word the message?

I expected to see the usual Sunday posts – we do this thing every Sunday where we share pictures of our babies and say what new things they've learned – but instead, I saw that same awful smiling mugshot of Rob and a link to the Lincolnshire Gazette. I didn't need to click on it – the headline glared at me. It read: 'Local Man Released From Custody Pending Further Investigations'.

I just made it to the toilet bowl before puking.

Rob was out. He was out of prison, or that little cell inside the station. Whatever. I wasn't thinking straight. I am still working for Caine Reynolds. *Still working for that piece of shit company and that horrible man is still my boss.*

And Rob was out of custody.

Rob was free, and I wasn't.

I was dripping wet; I didn't know whether it was from sweat or tears or sick. I laid my head on the toilet seat.

Come on, Jaime, think. Minutes must have passed.

I had no choice, there was no way I could pay back thirty thousand pounds. Thirty fucking thousand pounds. That's not exactly money that we had lying around. It would be more than both Oliver's and my savings accounts put together. I must go in. I must go back to that place, and face those people again. What is Niamh going to say?

I had no time to shower. I pulled Thursday's crumpled suit out of the laundry basket and attempted to wipe away yesterday's makeup, sweat, and sick residue with baby wipes. I looked like shit – I didn't need a full-length mirror to know that, but finding an ironed blouse or putting on deodorant was *way* down the list of my priorities right now.

I scanned around downstairs to make sure all the windows and doors were shut and ran out through the garage door. There was a large dried oil patch where Oliver's monstrous car usually sits.

I spent the entire twenty-minute car journey desperately trying to get hold of him using the car's dashboard phone.

"Hello, you are trying to reach me, Oliver..."
"Hello, you are trying to reach me, Oliver..."
"Hello, you are trying to—"
"ARGH!"

I was still shaking, and the threat of vomiting again was highly-likely when I got out of the lift on the sixth floor. I had resigned myself to the thought that I would just have to endure this bastard place for another two and a half months – I've already done two weeks – and promised myself that I would hand in my notice as soon as legally possibly, preferably while sticking two fingers up at Clive and Ryan.

Just two and a half more months. Just two and a half more months.

"Oh my god, you came in," said Rachel, jumping up from her seat at reception.

"Where's Clive?" I said, not making eye contact with her.

"He's in a client meeting in the boardroom. He told me to tell you, if you showed up, which he didn't seem to think was very likely, that you're are late for work, and for the meeting, and you should wait at your desk for a formal disciplinary." She looked at her shoes. "And that you will be receiving a formal investigation for your behaviour at the CRAPs, and that if you make one more mistake...you'll...uh...be fired. And if you are fired you will still have to pay back your mat pay." She bit her lip and held her hands out, palms up, as if to say there was nothing she could do. Of course there was nothing she could do. "I'll come and get you when he's out. I'm so sorry."

"It's fine." It was nothing less than I'd expected.

"Thank you, Rachel. I just want you to know that when I called you all a bunch of mouldy old cunts, I didn't mean you personally." I still couldn't make eye contact.

She gave a small, tinkling laugh, and sat back down at her desk. She began rifling through papers, but I had the feeling that she was merely play-acting, so she didn't have to talk to me anymore.

I turned on the spot and walked to the door of the Chamber. I paused. Who, beyond these walls, will have been personally offended by what I said? Possibly everyone – definitely Ryan. I closed my eyes and allowed four seconds to compose myself. I pushed the door open.

Somebody yelled, "Jaime's here," and then silence fell upon the room, quickly and completely, as if a radio had been turned off. Every single pair of eyes was on me, as I took my walk of shame up to Ryan's – thankfully empty – desk. No attempt was made by anybody to hide their glares; people were craning their necks to get a better view, even people in the offices that lined the walls had wheeled their chairs into the doorways. The horrifying realisation that I would have to take this walk every day, several times a day, for the next two and a half months was all around me like a swarm of wasps.

A slow rumbling of murmurs broke out. I concentrated on my feet and where I was walking, getting quicker and quicker. I dared not look at anyone. I caught snatches of whispered conversations: "mouldy bunch of cunts", "flipped off the partners", "Harry's got it all on YouTube already". I got to Ryan's desk and collapsed into the chair next to his, enveloping my head in my arms. I will just have to stay like this for two and a half months.

"Hun! I just heard, oh God, are you okay?" Niamh was there beside me, in Ryan's chair, and she flung her arms around me. "I can't believe they're making you do this. Well I can actually, because, you know."

I pushed my hair out of my face and peered at Niamh through my fingers. I wanted to talk about me, how unjust this all was that I would have to endure this spectacle every day, and how I was on the very verge of getting fired and would still have to pay the money back to this bastard firm. I wanted to apologise to Niamh for dangling her dream in front of her face and then pissing all over it, but when I looked into her eyes I could only think of one thing to say.

"He's out."

"What do you mean, sweetie?"

"That guy, my friend's husband; you know, the one that we got arrested on Friday. He's out of custody. What does that mean? Will he get charged or—"

"Well, well, well, look what the cat dragged in," said Ryan, smirking. He loomed over Niamh, almost pressing his genitals into her face. He tossed his client files on the desk.

"Oh fuck off, Ryan, nobody says 'look what the cat dragged in', are you some old man or something?" said Niamh.

He wagged his finger at Niamh and tutted; he was still smiling. "Now, now, that's ageist," he said. "You could get fired for that kind of discrimination. Imagine the irony. And that's my seat." He inched his crotch even closer to her face. "It's reserved for the Lawyer of the Year, and the next Caine Reynolds' partner, and I kindly ask that you fuck off and let your new boss sit down."

Niamh jumped out of the chair to look him directly in the eye. They had a sort of stare-out.

Ryan won. "Copy those, Jaime," he said, indicating to the files scattered across the desk.

There was no point in arguing. I scooped together the

envelopes and began to traipse towards the admin office on the other side of the floor with my head hung low. Niamh followed me.

The reception from the admin staff was just as warm as from the rest of the building. Thankfully, for now, Lauren was not in. Maybe she had called in sick, maybe she was on holiday. I didn't want to ask – I didn't think I had the energy to apologise anymore.

Niamh pulled Lauren's empty swivel chair up to the machine to keep me company while I silently copied Ryan's notes from his earlier client meetings. They were riddled with errors, spelling and clerical. *Urgh*. Clive's prodigious cadet, the future of this company. Did he know what was in that golden envelope all along? Was he being honest about the partner position? Surely not, for everyone's sake.

"Jaime. Ryan told me I'd find you here."

I near shat myself upon hearing Clive's voice. I forced myself to make eye contact with at least one of his eyes.

Niamh squeezed my arm and whispered, "I'll call you later hun." Then she left me standing at the copier alone with Clive. I guess this was all my fight.

He looked me up and down. His eyes following the creases of my clothes, to the stain on my jacket, to the absolute birds' nest of a mom-bun that was my hair.

"Hmm. I've got your return-to-work forms." He pushed a small stack of papers into my fist. "You'll also find invitations to your formal disciplinary hearings for both your behaviour on Friday evening and your tardiness today, I might also add your inexcusable attire. I've asked that Occy-Health be present at the hearings; I'm sure you'll agree that's reasonable, given your questionable mental wellbeing?"

I said nothing but closed my fingers around the papers.

We both knew that I had no intention of signing the forms. Now it was just a waiting game.

"I expect things to return to how they were," he continued, "except that Ryan will be in charge of the high-profile clients now, and for the time being you will be reporting to him. Don't take it personally, it's just a matter of what's best for the firm.

"You should also know that we've a three-strikes policy. And you're already up to two. So *please* don't give me any more ammo, OK?"

If he expected me to respond, he didn't wait for it. He turned on the spot and marched out of the admin office, pausing at the doorway long enough to say; "Oh, and Jaime, I want my golf clubs."

Without saying goodbye to anyone, including Niamh – I would text her later or wait for her to call – I left at midday to pick River up from nursery. After, I headed straight home. We would bunk swim class and Bounce and Sing – I wasn't in the right head space anyway. My phone was showing missed calls and voicemail notifications. I plugged it into the car's USB charger and played the messages through the speaker system.

"You have three new messages. First new message: message received today at 11:20 a.m.: "Jaime, it's Olly, what's wrong? I just got about a thousand messages from you all saying 'FUUUUCK'. Call me back."

"Second new message: message received today at 11:34 a.m.: "Jaime, call me back, are you OK? Is River OK? Where are you?"

"Third new message: message received today at 11:49 a.m.: "Jaime I'm leaving work now. Call. Me. Back. Now."

I pulled onto the drive, the garage doors lifting automatically. Oliver's car wasn't there yet; he was probably still on his way back. I drove into the garage and waited for the doors to slide down behind me, the fluorescent strip lights blinking on overhead. I turned the engine off, unplugged my phone and stuffed it back into my handbag. Behind me River was blowing raspberries.

My hand was on the car door handle. I paused. A shadow moved between the shelving units where we keep the tools and DIY stuff. A cat, maybe? Wouldn't be the first time a cat had got in. Next doors cat, Tyrion, was always breaking in through the kitchen window. The kitchen window, though… It would have had to come in through the internal garage door. Did I leave it open? My eyes flicked over to it – nope, it was closed – the shadow flickered again.

I snapped my head in the direction of the movement. It grew larger, taller, filling the whole space between the shelves. It inched forwards, gradually surfacing into the light, and a lumbering, hulking figure stepped into view. It was no cat.

Rob Sparks' body was rigid, his face red and blotchy, and his eyes were, unblinkingly, fixed on me.

CHAPTER EIGHT

He began yelling, his voice muffled through the glass and the sheer panic ringing through my head. I smashed my hand on the automatic door lock button, just in time – Rob's hand snatched at the passenger door handle. He wrenched at it several times, but the door remained firmly closed.

"GET OUT OF THE CAR! GET THE FUCK OUT OF THE CAR."

I couldn't see his face anymore, just his grubby white t-shirt. There was a deafening bang and the ceiling of the car crunched and bounced. He had hit it. I needed to get out of there. I hit the start button, thrusting my foot onto the clutch. The engine burst into life and the car was propelled inches forwards – it cut out and the steering wheel smashed me in the chest.

Rob jumped backwards. He grabbed something, a wrench I think, from the shelves behind him. I fumbled again with the start button. The fucking thing wouldn't go again. I alternated slamming my foot onto the clutch and gas. I was yelling now, too. The engine roared, and I thrust the car into reverse. There was a knack to getting the garage door to open from the inside of the car, but I didn't have time to try and remember, I just started driving. We lurched backwards, and there was a tremendous noise like a shopping trolley smashing through a window as we crashed heavily into the garage doors. I shot forward in my seat, smacking my forehead now on the steering wheel. I tried reversing again, the wheels spinning ferociously, but the boot thundered against the metal door. A sharp crack sounded, and the car stopped moving. I revved the engine, the smell of spent petrol and burning rubber crept in but nothing else happened.

I had barely a second to cover my face. Rob swung back his arm and lashed the front passenger window with the wrench. An ear-splitting ring, and tiny cubes of glass were projected inwards, completely showering me. River began wailing, gut-wrenching, agonising, screams, and I could only assume that she too had been covered in broken glass.

My priority now was to protect her, to jump in the back and cover her tiny body with mine, but before I could swing my leg around to climb over, Rob's hand shot into the car, closed around the back of my head, seized me by the hair, and with inhuman strength, he dragged me out of the car, through the broken window, and threw me onto the concrete garage floor.

Drops of blood mingled with the tiny shards of glass around me. My hair had been ripped out of my scalp by the roots – surely I could not have any left, though I knew this was false because Rob still had hold of me by it.

"Where is she?" he yelled.

He pushed my head downwards. I could see only his trainers and the bottom of his jeans – they were both muddy. I tried to move my head to look at River, but his grip was too strong. I couldn't speak, I only felt a crushing weight against my throat, even if I could I doubt he would have heard over River's screams.

"WHERE IS SHE?!"

He tightened his grip and pulled my head backwards so that I was forced to look into his contorted face.

"You did this! YOU! You fucking drugged me and got me arrested."

There was blood in my mouth, I swallowed it, I didn't want to show him how hurt I was. "I only wanted to talk to you at the races." My voice was even.

River's sobs had grown to the point where she was gagging. I bit my lower lip to keep me from screaming for her.

Again he hardened his grip on the back of my head, pulling it back further still, and crouched down in front of me, his face centimetres from mine.

"Tell me where I can find my wife," he hissed. His breath was hot, it stung the gashes on my face. "You owe me."

I wanted so badly to look at River, but I needed to keep his attention on me. At least until I figured out what to do. I closed my eyes.

"OPEN YOUR FUCKING EYES!" He shook me. "TELL ME!"

Fucking think, Jaime!

I scanned the floor with my peripherals, looking for some kind of weapon. I was hoping for big enough shard of glass, but it was all tiny cubes. I tried to visually remember everything in the garage: the placement of the tools, the layout, everything. Maybe I could shove a screwdriver into the side of his neck, if I could reach one.

"I don't know where she is," I said, stalling for time.

"Yes you fucking do. This is all *your* fault. You'll pay for messing in my shit. You and your stupid fucking friends. Erin. Kelly. And that fat redhead friend of yours. Don't even get me started on Ella, the little bitch."

How did he know these names?

"I'm not messing around," he spat. He grabbed my face with his free hand and pressed his own so close to mine that we could have been kissing, if it weren't for the awful angle he was pushing my body into. I tried to shove him away, get him off me, but he was as solid and unyielding as the concrete I was knelt on. He squeezed my jaw and turned my head towards River's window. She was coughing between sobs, and rasping on the intake breath. My heart was on fire; I couldn't get to her to protect her. I was failing her as a mother.

"You'll fucking pay for this," he said directly in my ear. "I'll start with the baby—"

There was a deafening screech and a crunch. The car shuddered and lurched upwards and then dropped back to the ground. Rob let go of my head and I toppled backwards, hitting the side of my face on the garage floor. Daylight was beginning to flood in. The door had freed itself of the car and was juddering back up.

"Jaime?" Oliver called from somewhere outside.

Rob's trainer grazed my cheek, and before I could push myself to my knees, he was gone; squeezed through the gap under the door and legged it.

Oliver's car was in the middle of the drive, the driver's side door open and Olly nowhere to be seen. He emerged moments later inside the garage, breathing heavily.

"Shit Jaime, what happened?" He scooped me up and took my face in his hands. His touch was gentle, and his eyes darted from one graze to another. "Are you OK?"

I didn't answer him. I shook him off and flung the rear passenger door open, and in one swift motion I unclipped and lifted out my screaming baby, sending more tiny cubes of glass to the floor, and brought her close to my chest. Her face and hair were soaked with tears, or sweat. I wanted to envelop her into my body, absorb her through osmosis, so that she could never be harmed by that monster, or anyone else ever again, but I did the only thing I knew would instantly calm her: I whipped my boob out and stuck it in her mouth. It always worked.

"We need to call the police," he said, taking his phone out of his pocket.

"That was Rob," I said.

Oliver whipped his head round to the spot where Rob had vanished, and then surveyed the carnage in the garage. Broken glass and droplets of blood littered the floor. The car was smashed in at the back and the garage door wouldn't open fully because the metal was blown out at the bottom. And then there was me, standing in the centre of the rubble and chaos, clothes ripped to shreds, blood all over my face and blouse, and a tiny baby nestled onto my tit.

"I'm gonna fucking kill him," he said.

I grabbed the phone from him and locked the screen. "No, *I'm* going to."

Oliver helped me clean and change River, and get her down for a nap. Luckily she was not badly harmed, only a few tiny scratches on her hands. Then he picked the glass out of my hair while I sat in the bath. My wounds, which were fewer than I had originally imagined, and mostly superficial, smarted in the warm bath water. They were concentrated on my arms, and the left side of my torso, where I had been dragged through the jagged window and thrown on the glass-strewn ground. There were patches where my hair had been ripped out by the roots, and if anything, they stung more than the cuts, and a large bruise was forming on the side of my forehead. My blouse was in the bathroom waste bin, though my skirt might be salvageable.

"It doesn't look too bad now," said Oliver when he was finished patting dry my hair. He had carefully brushed it over so that the bigger bald patches were hidden.

"It'll grow back," I said, inspecting it in the mirror. My hair did always have a knack of growing incredibly quickly.

"I'll just clean up the garage and then I'll put the kettle on," said Oliver.

I wanted to help, but I had a few more pressing things to sort out first. "I just want to take some photos, if that's OK?"

"Of course. Are you sure you don't want to call the police?"

I shook my head. There is absolutely no way I could involve the police. So that what, he could be arrested again and then let go? Of course, unlike Marie, I would press charges. I googled how long the prison sentence is for actual bodily harm: five years maximum, less with good behaviour. Less than five years for dragging me through a window, ripping out my hair, and threatening my baby. No. I needed something more...finite.

"It won't be enough," I said.

Olly nodded. He grabbed the baby monitor and we both headed downstairs.

I thought that I would show the other moms, rather than explain what I had planned. They wouldn't understand. If I just told them that I needed to kill Rob Sparks, they would think that I was crazy. No sane person just decides to murder someone, right?

But I kept thinking of the moment the window was blown in and glass covered River, the feeling of his hands ripping my hair from its follicles, and his hot rancid breath on my face. *I'll start with the baby.*

I'll start with the baby…

What would have happened if Oliver hadn't shown up at that exact time? Would he have hurt her? My daughter. Would he have killed her? What would he have done with me afterwards?

I'll start with the baby…

I kept reliving the moment in my mind, except this time I imagined a scenario in which I had stashed a knife in my bag. It would have been easy, in that moment, and a release, to plunge the thing into his chest and put an end to his tyranny.

He had known their names, too; my friends from the moms' group. Does he know where they live? Each of them has a baby River's age. None of them are safe now. And what about that poor girl, Ella – does he know that she's pregnant? She was rubbing her belly at the racecourse; I doubt she thought anyone noticed. Is that why he beat her last time?

I had drawn only one conclusion; this man must be stopped. He must be immediately and eternally stopped. And it must be me to do it.

I'm a Mamabear, protecting my cub.

I uploaded three pictures to the moms' group that night. They would see my motives with their own eyes. They might not agree with my decision, but at least they would understand. After all, it had been the photo of Marie's battered face that had spurred me into action before. Their safety was in jeopardy, and their babies' – perhaps they would even want to help me.

The first photo I posted was of my work blouse laid out on the bathroom floor. The cream silky fabric had been bloodily shredded on the left side and, on the right, there were tiny perfect holes where shrapnel had hit me. It looked like the blouse was covered in cigarette burns. In the force of being pulled from the window the neckline had been ripped out of shape and the top buttons were yanked away, just some blood-soaked thread dangling where they once were.

The second picture was of the car and the garage floor: the cragged, bloody window, the smashed in bumper, the garage door, and the glass cubes like glitter covering everything.

I sobbed as I uploaded the final picture, but by the time I hit send, I was awash with a resounding determination to fix it. The picture was of River's rear-facing car seat, which was largely unscathed – but pooled in the bottom of the seat was a sea of broken glass. It looked as if I had scooped glass up off the ground and thrown it into the seat for dramatic effect, but if anything, most of the shards covering my baby were lost to the garage floor when I pulled her out.

I captioned the photos with 'He knows where I live and he has your names, none of you are safe. He threatened River. Tomorrow I will stop him once and for all.' Then I added, 'Let me know if you'd like to join me,' as if I were doing no more than planning a picnic. I didn't bother to ask what they thought I should do, whether they could think of a better way to deal with it, without resorting to murder, or ask why I didn't just call the police. I didn't want to invite debate, or even sympathy, I just needed them to know why. I had made my mind up. Maybe I would even turn off the comments – but they began to pour in.

Carys Honeyman - 16th March - 19:04
How did he find out where you live? I'm definitely coming. Let me know where and when.

Kelly Vaughan -16th March - 19:04
Definitely in. I thought we should've done it in the beginning.

Molly Cheung - 16th March - 19:06
I can get the train up. I need to see him stopped.

Ruchi Kapoor - 16th March - 19:07
Yes. I'm in. We need a plan though, I don't want to go to prison.

Jaime Wright - 16th March - 19:08
I didn't expect you all to be on board with it. I have a plan, but if it goes tits up I'll take the fall. There is one thing I need help with though. I need help finding him.

Erin Schellenger - 16th March - 19:11
I think I know someone that can help. Give me a minute.

Jeanie Gillespie - 16th March - 19:13
For real are you talking about killing someone?

. . .

Jaime Wright - 16th March - 19:14
  Yes.

Jaime Wright - 16th March - 19:14
  Are you coming or not?

Jeanie Gillespie - 16th March - 19:15
  Absolutely. Wouldn't miss that for the world.

Erin Schellenger - 16th March - 19:34
  Apparently, he's working cash-in-hand under his brother's name at a timber yard about 30 minutes outside the city. He should be there at 9 tomorrow, if he turns up for work that is.

Jaime Wright - 16th March - 19:38
  Good sourcing Erin, thanks. I'm going to hire a minibus. Everyone that wants to come I will pick up from New Street at 8:30.

Marie Sparks - 16th March - 19:46
  I'm not going to say anything, except that I can't be there.

"I'm coming with you," said Oliver.

I had set up camp for us in the living room, River in a travel cot and Olly on the sofa with a blanket. I took the armchair by the window so I could peer out onto the drive every twenty minutes or so.

"Absolutely not, this is something *I* have to do. And I

need you to stay home with River. Can't take a baby on a manhunt – don't be stupid."

"Well drop her off to nursery and then we'll go together. I'm not letting you go alone."

"I'm not going alone; my mom friends are coming with me. Plus, what happens if we both get arrested for murder? Who will look after River if we're both serving life sentences? Your mom? Over my dead body."

Oliver rolled his eyes like he did every time I bitched about Colleen, and temporarily gave up trying to coax me. Every ten minutes or so he alternated between asking if I wanted him to come and asking if I wanted to involve the police. Each time I shook my head. Eventually, at about 1 a.m., he began snoring. Perhaps he thought that by the morning I would have changed my mind.

I spent the rest of the night on the edge of sleep, stirring at every single unfamiliar noise, convinced that Rob would try to break in and finish the job. He must know that I would tell someone; maybe he thought I would call the police, maybe he'd gone into hiding again. It would make tracking him down tomorrow slightly trickier, but that's something I'd deal with then. If he was not at the timber yard we could stake out his brother's house, if Erin can find the address. He has to show his face at some point, and I'm convinced that ugly red sofa belongs to Bradley.

I half-hoped to have an uneventful night and get some rest, and half-hoped Rob would show up so that I could stab him on the driveway and then bury him under the conifers. It's a well-shaded area – not much chance of being overlooked. At one point during the night I was certain I saw something, a man maybe, bearing the hereditary Sparks' shoulders and haunch, sitting on the bottom wall, but perhaps it was just a trick of the moonlight, because when I moved to the porch to get a better look he was no longer there.

At around 4:30 a.m., before Oliver and River woke, I got up and packed an 'assassinator's bag' to take with me. Since I wouldn't have time to go to B&Q in the morning to buy supplies, I improvised with items we had around the house: IKEA scissors from the 'everything drawer'; Marigolds from under the kitchen sink; Gaffer Tape from the garage; plastic dust proof sheeting left over from decorating the hall; lighter fluid and a flick lighter left over from last summer's BBQ supplies, in case I needed to burn any evidence; and the biggest, baddest, sharpest, kitchen knife I could find. The one we usually saved for hacking up sweet potatoes. I did a few practice plunges into thin air. I couldn't help feeling that I was missing something though.

Then I went upstairs and got dressed in black leggings and a long-sleeve black t-shirt. I stuffed a spare set of black clothes into a carrier bag and an old, long, white Smiffy wig from when I dressed as Storm three Halloweens ago.

I gave River a kiss on the forehead and slipped a note under Oliver's cushion pillow which said 'See you later, hopefully.' It was easier than saying goodbye – what if he tried to stop me? What if I tried to stop myself?

I slung the holdall over my shoulder and slipped out of the door into the bracing March dawn. My Picasso wasn't in any fit state to drive, and I didn't want to take Oliver's muscle car – far too conspicuous, and traceable – so I walked the four or five miles to the nearest car rental garage.

My breath fogged in the air, and with every exhale I felt clearer, more focused; like the steam was the anxiety and trepidation leaving my body. It was not something you ever expect yourself to be doing – getting up at dawn to go on a murderous, vigilante mission, but there I was, knife, tape, plastic sheeting in tow, ready to hunt down a man, and go full Mamabear on his ass.

"Hello, I'd like a minibus please, for, like, right now," I said to the receptionist, walking into the tiny rental office the moment it opened at 8 a.m.

"Uh, yeah sure, have you got your driver's licence?" The receptionist was young, late teens, or early twenties. She wore her hair in a tight ponytail, and she spoke with a thick Brummie accent. She looked me up and down, but when she spoke to me, she avoided staring straight into my eyes, preferring to look at a spot about six inches to the left of my ear; a nervous tic probably. A good thing for me, hopefully she won't remember the details of my face.

I handed over my driving licence and debit card. There was no way to avoid the minibus being in my name. Perhaps if I'd had longer to organise this I could have asked Kelly if she knew where to get fake documents – she seemed like she would know this kind of thing – but it was either now, or chicken out, so it had to be now. I would just need to make sure that wherever we killed him there would be no CCTV to connect the minibus to the murder.

She glanced at my licence, and then handed me a form to fill out.

"We've got a sixteen-seater, is that any good?"

I nodded.

"Is it for a hen do?"

"Not quite," I said, scribbling my name in the box.

"Oh good, because we have to charge more for hen and stags because of the extra cleaning," said the receptionist. "Come with me and we can do an inventory check."

She led me out through the back into the yard area and walked up to a white minibus with tinted windows. She leafed through the documents that I had just signed and found the page she was looking for.

"Right, here is a list of all the dings and scratches. Walk with me around the van and let me know if you see any more."

We began walking around the van, hunched over like those figures from the 'caution – elderly people crossing' signs. She pointed to different parts on the bus, but I wasn't listening, I was thinking about Rob – and there was something else I needed to do...

"And there's another one there…Oh and that's quite a big one there…"

"Excuse me, I've just remembered I need to make a phone call," I said, standing up straight.

The receptionist straightened up, too. She sighed, like doing her job was all such a big inconvenience, but she didn't say anything.

I took my phone out of my bra – my leggings were somewhat lacking on the pocket department – and brought up work's number.

"Hello, Caine Reynolds," said Rachel's pleasant voice.

"Hi Rachel, can you put me through to Clive please?" I looked at the receptionist, pointed at the phone, and mouthed "work."

The receptionist nodded and began rubbing at the closest ding with her finger.

"Clive Ross."

"Hi Clive, it's Jaime. I'm not coming into work today. I've got the runs."

"Bloody hell, Jaime you can't just call in sick, you're already on two stri—"

"I SAID I'VE GOT THE RUNS!" I screamed. I

pressed the end call button and stuffed the phone back in my bra. "Sorry about that go on," I said to the receptionist, who now seemed to be choking on something.

I pulled up to New Street station at bang on 8:30. There was a group of six or seven moms waiting for me, all dressed in some interpretation of Hollywood movie ninjas. Some of them had car seats with babies in.

WTF? Why had they brought their babies? They do realise what we're going to do today?

They waved and smiled at me, as I reversed into the loading bay, clearly all very excited to be going on this 'little jaunt'. Standing on the side of the road they looked like a bunch of overgrown kids, waiting for the school coach to pull up and take them swimming.

I found the door button and pushed it down; it hissed, and slid to the side.

"TICKETS PLEASE," I said by way of greeting them. I wasn't nearly as nervous to meet them as I was when we went to the races. In fact, I think I might actually be enjoying this trip so far, except for the tag-along babies. And it would be lovely to see Kelly, Erin and Carys again and meet a few of the new moms.

"Sorry," said Kelly piling onto the bus, tripping on the step in. She was the first mom to have brought her baby. "It's just... I couldn't get childcare this last-minute. She can stay on the bus, while we... you know. She'll be as good as gold."

"It's OK," I found myself saying, despite the fact that it really wasn't.

Kelly went straight to the back of the bus, just like all the bad girls from school.

The next mom on was visually impaired Molly Cheung. She was carrying her white stick, though she evidently had left her baby – I struggled to remember what he was called… Jack? Jacob? – at home with her partner, in… Weston-super-Mare? That rang a bell.

"Hi, Jaime, it's so good to meet you finally," she said in her soft West Country accent. She took the seat directly behind my driver's one.

Next on came Erin. "Hey, how are you feeling?" She grabbed my arm by the elbow and gave me a kiss on the forehead. "Alright if I sit here with you Molly? I've got the directions to the timberyard on my phone."

"Not at all, it'll be lovely to sit with you," said Molly.

The next mom on was Ruchi from London. She must have gotten on the train at about six this morning to be here. She had a car seat with her baby in; I was pretty sure that he was called Eshwar. It was hard remembering all the babies' names, and other facts about the moms, without the pinned introduction posts and map that I'd become accustomed to on the group.

"Well, this is exciting," she said giving me a hug.

"Thanks for coming," I said. A lump began to form in my throat, and I got that feeling where you don't quite know which emotion you're experiencing but you know you probably want to cry. It was the scale of the support I was being shown that was overwhelming me. Of course, the support was for Marie too, but I was, literally, in the driver's seat here.

Ruchi took a seat in the middle of the bus, strapping the baby in by the window.

Then came Jeanie. She was an older mum in her mid-forties, with a teenage daughter, as well as a nine-month-old which, to my dismay, she had brought too.

"Hi Maddison," I said looking at the teenager; at least

I'd remembered her name. I turned to Jeanie. "Um...are you sure this is a good idea bringing her, like, did you tell her what's going to happen? What we're going to do?" I whispered the last bit.

"Yes of course, she can't wait," said Jeanie.

Contrary to what Jeanie had said, Maddison skulked to the back of the bus, sat next to Kelly, pulled out her phone and immediately zoned out.

"Teenagers," said Jeanie, and she took the seat at the front, across the aisle from Erin and Molly.

Lastly came Carys, who had not brought her baby. She sat in the seats between Ruchi and Erin, with her legs draped into the aisle.

"OK, is that everyone?" I yelled. I pressed the button again and the doors hissed closed.

The small amount of excited buzz that had broken out between the moms immediately stopped. Everyone was staring at me. I hadn't really planned on giving any kind of speech, but I could feel an expectation of one brewing.

"Before we get going, I would just like to thank you all for your support today on this, and, yeah, so here's the plan."

Out loud it felt foolish to say. The eyes of the moms, and Maddison, bore into me. Some of the faces were smiling, some looked concerned, some slightly distracted by the babies, who, at this point at least, were all still very well-behaved.

"I have a step-by-step plan," I said, trying to project my voice right to the back of the bus. "Step one: we drive to the timber yard. Step two: we find Rob and stalk him and wait for him to be alone with no CCTV cameras, or anything around him. Step three: I stab him through the heart. Step four: we bundle the body into some plastic sheets that I have in my bag. Step five: we weigh him down and dump him in the canal. Does anyone have any questions?"

Carys' hand went up. I guess it was a school trip. "Are we bringing the body back onto the bus?"

"Uh, yeah I guess so, otherwise we won't have any way to get him to the canal."

Carys nodded and bit her thumb nail.

I added, "We can just lie him in the centre here." I pointed to the aisle like an air stewardess.

"What if we can't get him on his own?" Kelly yelled from the back, just passing over the fact that in a few short hours there may be a dead body in the aisle of the bus.

"Then we'll lure him," I said.

"How?" shouted Kelly.

"I'll use myself as bait," I said.

"If he chases after you, and you can't stab him, I'll stab him in the back," said Kelly. "I've brought my own knife."

"Me too," said Carys.

"Yes, I did too," said Jeanie.

"OK but we don't want to stab him too many times, or there'll be too much blood, and I stupidly didn't bring anything to clean it up with," I said.

"I've got wet wipes!" said Ruchi, optimistically.

"What if he's not at the wood place?" said Molly.

It was Erin that jumped in. "If he's not at the timber yard, then I think I know Bradley's – his brother's – address."

"What if you chicken out?" said Ruchi. "Do you want us to stab him then?"

"Um...I'm going to try my very best not to chicken out."

On the way, and after a few recitals of 'The Wheels on the Bus' for the benefit of the babies, we decided collectively that it would be best if I parked away from the timberyard and we walked to the office to check for Rob, in case there was any CCTV. We didn't want the number plate of the mini bus recorded on anything, and also I really wanted to keep all of the babies as far away from the murdering as I could.

Erin, Jeanie, and Kelly made the walk with me to the office, which turned out to be a small converted shipping container, and Carys would follow in the bus if need be. I had managed to cram all my hair into the long white-blonde wig, even though the other moms laughed at me.

Erin and Jeanie waited outside of the front entrance – lookouts - and Kelly and I walked inside. There were a couple of desks and some filing cabinets pushed up to one side of the container, a sleeping greyhound on a sofa on the other side, and a door, swung wide open on the far end.

"Helloooo?" I called. "Anybody there?" A quick once-over told me that there were no cameras in this office. If Rob were to turn up right now it would be an ideal stabbing spot: secluded, surrounded by woodland, relatively soundproof. The one problem I could foresee with this would be the clean-up, and maybe the dog too; not sure how it would behave.

A few seconds into my mental preparations a man walked in through the open back-door, he had a long beard that went into a little plait at the end, and he carried a tape measure and a teeny little pencil that he had probably nicked from Screwfix or IKEA. He jumped when he saw us.

"Can I help?" He had a Blackcountry accent, very

subtly different, but you can tell if you're from around here.

"We're looking for my partner," I said. We had decided that partner was more believable than friend or relative.

"And who's that?" said the man, setting down his things.

"Um…" Oh bugger. I looked at Kelly. It was Rob's brother, what was he called again? "Bradley. Bradley Sparks."

"Bradley Sparks?" said the man, with a slight shake of his head. "You mean the feller with the bulldog tattoo? I've not seen him since Thursday, sorry."

Crap. It was plan B then. I could have asked him for Bradley's address, but I didn't want to give him anything to tell the police, and besides if Rob was working cash-in-hand they probably don't keep records of these things anyway.

"Ok, thanks," I said, and the two of us left the container office and joined Erin and Jeanie outside.

"Do you think he was telling the truth?" asked Jeanie, when we relayed what the man had said.

"I think so," I said.

Kelly nodded her agreement.

"What now?" said Erin.

"I don't know, maybe we should try his brother's. You think you know his address? Let's just get back to the bus and tell the others."

The three moms and I marched back through the muddy, twiggy path to the bus, which was parked in a layby in a copse a few hundred metres from the timberyard perimeter.

All the moms that had remained on the bus had gathered in the front section, staring out of the window at us. As we got closer, we could make out Carys hovering over the driver's seat and ferociously pointing out of the window, through the trees, to a spot up a nearby hill.

All four of us turned to look. There, trundling along the hillside, silhouetted against the morning sun and rapidly reducing the distance between himself and the bus, was Rob.

He was dressed for outdoors work, wearing a grey check shirt, blue jeans, and heavy steel-toe-capped boots that were noisily snapping twigs as he moved. He was engrossed in his phone, his shoulders hunched over and his head bent low looking at the screen. He crossed the space in the woods quickly and finally stepped out into the road about 40 feet ahead of the bus. The other moms, with the exception of Molly, who had waited with Maddison and the babies, had all tumbled out and joined us on the muddy verge.

He looked up from his phone, clocked the bus, and then did a double-take as he spotted the six-woman strong welcome party.

Immediately he turned on the spot and stomped towards us. He was smiling, but it was the same cruel, vacant smile I had seen him wearing in his wanted photo in the paper.

"You stupid bitch," he spat. He was looking at me, and only me. "What the fuck do you think you're doing?" He stopped walking leaving a good twenty feet between us. Maybe he felt intimidated by the number of women waiting for him.

Good, see how you fucking like it.

This was it then. I suppose it was a good spot for murdering. I knew from earlier that there were no cameras in this patch of road. Hopefully no other cars would come during. Didn't need any witnesses. Or perhaps I could make him chase me deeper into the woods and then kill him there. I patted down my jeans pockets.

"Shit, I left my knife on the bus," I ventriloquist-whispered to the group beside me.

There was some shuffling amongst the moms, and someone pushed the hilt of a knife into my lower back. It was Kelly, I could tell from the coconut smell of her shampoo. I reached my hand back and my fingers closed around a wooden handle. I had no way of judging how big the knife was, how long it was, how wide the blade – was it serrated? I hoped not. I wanted a clean job.

He was inching closer. He had turned his body slightly sideways and held his arms aloft like a praying mantis. He looked like a boxer getting ready to spar. Did he know what I had planned? Was it a conscious decision, borne from experience maybe, to turn his body away, protect his vital organs? It would certainly make it more difficult to get a clear shot at his heart.

I took a single step forward. The other moms followed suit.

"Do you think I'm scared? A bunch of girls. Have you found me to teach me a lesson?"

Do it, Jaime, do it now. He could have killed you. He could have killed your friend. He could have killed your daughter. He's a monster. He deserves this. What you've got planned is too nice, as far as murders go... Just run up and stab him in the heart. He won't be expecting it, it'll be easy.

If I had a gun... Or maybe I should have poisoned him... Just as we had slipped GHB into his beer, we could easily have slipped him some rat poison or something. What was I thinking?

He inched closer still, turning his body even further to the side. He closed his fists. He was getting ready to fight us.

He knew. He knew what I had planned; that we had come to silence him. His eyes flicked across each of the moms, and came to rest again on me and my concealed arm.

Do it, Jaime, just do it now. He'll kill you otherwise.

The moms next to me were beginning to get restless. I felt very aware of their feet shuffling, their positions jostling. If I couldn't do it, would one of the others be able to?

Do it now, Jaime.

He was six feet away from me. And we were retreating. Tiny shuffles backwards. No, this wasn't how this happened.

NOW, JAIME! DO IT NOW!

I lunged forward, brandishing the knife, but at that very moment I knew that I had hesitated too long. I couldn't do it. Rob's left hand shot out and smacked the knife out of my hand. It thudded onto the road, slid down the camber and into the gutter on the other side. Milliseconds later his right hand shot forwards, fist clenched, and connected with my face. I was catapulted backwards through the air and landed in a heap in the mud. Blood erupted from my nose and gushed down my throat gagging me. I pushed myself back to my feet, siphoning off the blood with my sleeve.

Rob had lunged and grabbed the fallen knife before any of the moms could. He stood in the centre of a rapidly-expanding half circle of women, brandishing the knife at each of them in turn.

Carys, who was closest to the road, was making eye contact with me and raising her eyebrows in an odd way. She was trying to communicate something – but what? I saw a silver handle of a knife tucked into her belt loop, at the same moment that Rob spotted it too. He jumped forward, his enormous hand closed around Carys' arm and he spun her so that she was forced into his body. The blade of the first knife firmly held against her neck. Would he kill her? Or was she hostage?

None of us had a plan, least of all Rob, but I couldn't wait around to see what would happen.

"GET BACK IN THE VAN!" I screamed.

The moms scattered outwards.

Carys flung her body downwards, away from the knife, swinging herself and Rob around into an odd position. This was my chance. I grabbed the first thing I could see, an enormous 3-inch-thick tree branch, and I ran forward, with all the strength I could muster in those short seconds, and ploughed it into the small of Rob's back.

He was projected forward, his grip on Carys slackened and they both fell, face first, to the ground. Rob's chin hit the tarmac and the knife flew out of his hand and slid across the road. I heaved the branch back as far as I could and brought it down again between his shoulder blades. He splatted, cartoon-like, his face struck the road once again, and he remained mostly still. I pulled Carys from underneath his arm and together we pelted towards the bus. I could have stabbed him right then, but my body had switched from fight to flight.

The other moms had clambered on, I pushed Carys up the steps and threw myself into the driver's seat. I slammed my hand on the doors closed button and started the engine. Rob was pushing himself to his feet; he was shaky and slow, it looked like he might be disorientated. This was a stupid plan, and I was a fucking moron. I put myself, and my friends in danger. I've just got to get us away now. Hopefully a smack in the back with a big stick taught him a lesson and he'd leave us alone. If not, I'd get the police involved and let them deal with it all, and if I must do time for assault then so be it. I fumbled with the gearstick and jabbed it into reverse. Rob was on his feet and lumbering through the gutter towards the bus.

"GO, GO, GO, GO!" screamed Erin, smacking the back of the driver's seat.

Looking in the rear-view mirror, I hit the accelerator all the way down. The bus lurched a foot backwards, hissed and banged, and then shot several metres forward. With an incredible smacking crunching noise, the bus flattened Rob and bounced all the way over the top of his body. Moms were sent flying about in their seats and into the aisle, and the babies woke up and began to cry.

"I had it in first!" I yelled. "Fuck!" I slammed the bus into reverse, for real this time, and hit the accelerator. If I'd have given myself a second to think about it, I would have put two and two together and realised what was going to happen – but I didn't. I didn't do it on purpose, honestly. The van bounced back over Rob.

Thunk. Thunk. Thunk.

That was the different parts of his body hitting the underside of the minibus. Moms that had just picked themselves up out of the aisle were thrown back.

"FUCK, FUCK, FUCK!"

I slammed on the brakes, and stared, open-mouthed, out of the windscreen. Rob lay face down in the gutter a few metres from us. He didn't look very bloody, but he did look very dead.

My breathing became erratic. I threw open the window to try and get some air.

The moms, who were now getting to their feet for a second time, all clambered to the front to get a good look at him.

"Is he dead?" said Maddison.

. . .

Kelly pushed to the front, pressed the doors-open button and jumped out. I followed her; a few other moms climbed out, too.

Tentatively, we walked up to him. I watched closely for signs of movement, staring at his back, waiting for it to rise and fall, watching his hands and feet, waiting for a spasm of movement. But he was completely still.

I caught my trainer under his arm and flicked it upwards. It thudded back to the ground lifelessly.

A stick came from behind me, wielded by Ruchi, and poked him hard in the back. He didn't move.

More sticks appeared all around me and poked him everywhere. I was vividly reminded of the one time when we found a fox carcass in the playground at primary school.

I leaned over and touched his arm. He was warm, but I could not feel a pulse beneath his shirt cuffs. "I think he's dead."

"Good." Kelly jogged across the road and grabbed the knife. She crossed back and held it under his nose for a few seconds. The knife did not fog up.

"I think so too." She pushed him with her boot. "Should I stab him to make sure?"

"No," I said, throwing out my arm. "We'll leave him like this, maybe we can pass it off as a hit and run. Let's go, let's get out of here now, before anyone sees."

We ran back to the van. I managed the correct gear first time and we sped off down the road.

"That was fucking cool," said Maddison.

"Language!" yelled Jeanie, though she laughed and held her in a tight hug. The babies were beginning to settle again.

"I think I need a coffee," said Erin.

"I need wine," said Molly.

"OK, there's a garden centre not far from here," I said. "We could stop there for a bit, clean up and regain our composure. It has a soft play too."

Because what else would a bunch of moms do when they meet up but have coffee and go to soft play?

First, though, we had to clean the minibus. All we had were wet wipes, so we each took a few and set to work on a small section of the bus. For running over a man twice, there wasn't too much blood or other signs of impact, though we couldn't say for sure what the underside of the van looked like. We tied the wet wipes up in nappy bags and disposed of them in those rank nappy bins in the garden centre loos, along with my now pink wig. Erin also helped me to wipe the crusted blood off my own face.

"I think it's broken," she said, gently patting the top of my nose. "You're probably going to have two black eyes as well."

That'll look great for work. Wonder if Clive would try and fire me for that?

Aside from the murdering that had just happened, it really could have been any old moms' meet. We discussed *that* Game of Thrones ending and Bake Off, what words our babies can almost say; what birth control we are now using; who's TTC and who's pregnant again; where we're going on holiday; who we've had to block from the old group because they post too much bollocks on their ForumFriends wall; and, of course what we had planned for Mother's Day, this coming Sunday, as for many of us – myself included – it would be our first ever.

"We're just going to stay at home and have a roast I think," I said.

"Oh, us too," said Erin. "I've just learnt how to cook a proper British roast."

"I saw your vlog on that actually, it was hilarious," said Carys.

I sat back and watched my friends chatting. It was because of me they were here, not just here in the soft play on the cheesy-feet sofas drinking insipid lattes, but here together as friends. I was the one who set the group up almost a year ago, after it all kicked off on the main group. I was the one who insisted that we kept our much smaller group going, that we kept in touch, so that we could share the tough times – because I knew there'd be plenty.

I sipped my latte and sighed. Yeah, sure, we just committed murder and left the guy's body in the road for some poor jogger or dog walker to find, and sure, the police were probably looking for me right now, not to mention that BMW wanker who'll probably want to take me to court, and sue me for everything I have. At least if I was in prison I wouldn't have to go back to Caine Reynolds and deal with Clive or Ryan.

"What happens now? With our little lumberjack friend?" said Molly, interrupting my musings.

"I guess we wait," I said. "Somebody will discover his body sooner or later and call the police."

"I expect that, before long," whispered Erin, "it'll be in the news. Something like 'man found dead in hit and run'."

"That would be the best outcome," said Molly.

We sipped our coffees and nodded. The alternative was that the police suspected foul play, but I would deal with that if, and when, it arose.

Later, I dropped the group back to the railway station. There was much hugging, and cheek-kissing, and agreeing that it had been fun, and we ought to meet up again soon.

I checked the local news websites on my phone before I left the station, and again before I left the car rental place after dropping back the bus. Nothing yet. Had anyone found him? I wasn't stupid enough to phone in with a tip-off, but I desperately wanted to, just so that I could have the closure already.

It was about 6:30 p.m., when I walked through the door that night. Oliver was at the kitchen table with River. He caught sight of me.

"Shit babe, your face!"

"Do you like it?" I joked without smiling. I raised my hand to my nose and tested out the bridge with different gauges of pressure. It felt crunchy and very sore. "Is the news on yet?"

"Haven't you seen it?" he said in a tone that made me rush to the TV in the living room.

Just in time, the national news was finishing, and the local news was just beginning.

"Good evening, and welcome to Midlands Live. The latest tonight: Police are appealing for witnesses after a man was seriously injured during a hit and run incident earlier today."

Seriously injured?!

My mouth fell open. I turned to look at Oliver. "Fucks sake, fucker's still alive!"

CHAPTER NINE

We watched the rest of the report together.

"The man, whose identity has not yet been made public, is rumoured to have been released from police custody only yesterday. Police are particularly interested in speaking to two women, believed to have been in the area at the time of the incident." I looked at Oliver, my eyes wide. "The women are thought to be in their early twenties, one woman who was approximately five-foot, and the other about five-foot-five, both with long blonde hair."

Oliver side-eyed me.

The report continued: "It is thought that the man was on his way to Blackwood Timber Yard when he was struck by a vehicle. He was taken to Queen Elizabeth hospital earlier this morning, where he remains in an induced comatose state."

Oliver blinked at me.

"HA!" I exclaimed. "Early twenties, brilliant. Try thirty-four mate!" I marched out of the living room, and up the stairs.

Oliver chased after me with River in his arms.

"What are you going to do now?" he asked.

"I'm going to get changed, and then I'm going to finish the job. Can you help me cover up this?" I indicated to the area around my eyes, which was feeling more and more swollen with each passing minute.

"Um, yeah OK, but don't you think you should have some food first? Maybe a bath?"

"No time, babe. Anyway, I'm not hungry. I had a panini and a muffin in the garden centre." I pulled off my t shirt and leggings, wincing as the fabric rubbed over the glass cuts on my side, and threw them into the washing basket. "Can you put those on to wash when I'm gone? Erase the evidence."

"Jaime, what exactly did you do today?"

"Well... I'll tell you when I get back, though... actually, it's probably good thing that you don't know any details, it will make it more real if the police interrogate you."

I rifled through the cupboard and pulled out a pair of grey woollen trousers, a white cami, and a white chiffon blouse – my most doctorly-looking clothes.

I sat at the dresser and dabbed concealer under my eyes, adding layer after layer until I looked semi-normal again. There was no covering the puffiness; perhaps I could wear glasses. I half-wished I had another wig.

"How do I look?" I said standing up, scooping my feet into my grey kitten heels.

"Boneable," said Oliver.

"Well, maybe when I get back... If I get back."

I marched down the stairs, and again Oliver followed with River.

"Jaime?"

"I'll see you later babe. Love you so hard." I gave him a long kiss. "Bye my gorgeous little princess, see you in the morning." I planted a big kiss on top of River's head, winked at Oliver and walked out of the house, grabbing his blue, Birmingham City Council lanyard from the table next to the door on the way.

"JAIME?"

I had a remarkable, supportive husband. Not many women can say that their husbands would be so open about such things as homicide. I just hoped he'd support me a little longer, as I popped open the door on his restored 1966 A Code Ford Mustang Coupe. His first born. I turned the key and the engine roared into life. I could just picture his face, and the swears he might have chosen as he heard the familiar thundering noise of his hijacked baby. I backed out of the garage, down the drive and onto the road, as quickly as I could. Maybe I just imagined it, but I swore I glimpsed his red face at the porch window before I sped off.

Who else would be at the hospital? Rob's name had not been released to the public, but would the hospital staff know who he was? Would they have called any of his family to let him know he was there? Was I potentially going to walk into a room filled with the family of a man I put there? Holy shit, would Marie be there?

It was getting later now – perhaps visiting hours were over anyway. I could come back in the dead of night, less people around. That was both a good and a bad thing; less people meant that I wouldn't as easily be seen, but it also meant that there could be no blending into the crowd. I could always pull the fire alarm if there were people in the room, and then slip inside after they had evacuated. That could work.

I parked the car as far from the hospital building as possible and waited only a few moments before I went inside. There was a single receptionist at the front desk, immersed in conversation with what appeared to be a visitor. The clock above the desk read 8:45 p.m. It was the night shift; skeleton staff. I spotted a stack of ring binders on the desk and walked up to them. Confidently, I leaned forward and picked one up. The receptionist's eyes flicked down to the lanyard I was wearing. I had turned the photo ID card into my torso to hide Oliver's hirsute face – from this distance the lanyard may have passed for an NHS one. She acknowledged me with a quick smile and a nod, but did not take her attention away from the visitor. I marched away, down the dimly-lit corridor, my heels click-clacking on the grey screed and echoing across the walls.

I made sure never to lift my head, not once. I kept it down, immersed in the ring binder I had just picked up. I knew for sure that there would be CCTV cameras around the reception desks, lifts and possibly on the entrances to the wards – who could say where else they might be? I permitted myself a momentary glance at the department information board: critical care was on the second floor. I pushed the button for the lift and pretended to read my file.

Two junior doctors dressed in pink scrubs got in the lift, they smiled benignly at me and immediately resumed their conversation. One of them had gotten a kitten at the weekend, or something, I think it was called Xavier, though that might have been the doctor.

The lift doors pinged open, and all three of us stepped out. I followed the doctors along the corridor, hoping that they would lead me into the critical care ward, as I wouldn't be able to buzz myself in with Oliver's useless lanyard. Once we had reached the doors to the unit however, the junior doctors continued walking straight down the corridor and away from me.

Damn.

I stood in front of the double doors and took a deep gulp of air. He was in there, somewhere, and now I was going to kill him... again. I pressed the intercom button, remembering to keep my head down.

"Visiting times are over," said a crackly voice through the speaker.

"Doctor Rees, here to see Mr. Sparks. My card's not working for some reason." Doctor Rees was actually the surgeon that had performed my c-section, but it's a common surname, there must be more than one, and it was the first name that came to mind.

There was no reply, just a harsh reverberating buzz and a click from the door. I pushed it open and ploughed ahead. There were nurses at the desk, but they did not look at me; they seemed absorbed in their own due diligence. Again, I kept my head down, though I felt fairly certain there would be no cameras inside the ward because of patient privacy, I didn't risk it all the same. I searched for Rob's name on the whiteboard.

SPARKS B14

Following the signage on the room doors, I tried to not make eye contact with any of the nurses or other patients. B14 turned out to be, thankfully, a private room off a long glass corridor overlooking a slightly weedy courtyard. The blinds were drawn on the windows looking inwards, and it looked like the lights were off too. I knocked twice on the door with my knuckle. There was no response. I pushed the door ajar and peered in.

A shard of light from the corridor fell upon the bed, directly through the centre and onto its occupant. A waffle-patterned blanket had been pulled up to his neck. His head was still hidden behind the bed's privacy blinds. I strode around the bed, so that his head slowly came into view and stopped level with his feet. For someone who had just been run over twice by a minibus he sure didn't look like it. There were a few small scratches on his chin and cheek, but no bones seemed to be poking out or facing the wrong way; you could be mistaken for thinking he was just having a little nap. The door closed and the light from the corridor vanished. I screwed my eyes up to quickly adjust them to the darkness.

I didn't want to stare into his face too long. He was too vulnerable, oddly childlike. I wasn't going to hesitate like I did last time. Knowing my mistake now, I wasn't prepared to make it all over again. I moved around a bit farther, so that I was now squashed between his head and the horrid, uncomfortable blue armchair next to the bed.

It was that I saw him as a person. That was my mistake. He wasn't a person, he was inhuman, a monster. Perhaps this makes me one too, but I'm not the one threatening people's babies.

One look behind the bed told me that he was connected to an oxygen tank, an IV drip, a stats monitor, and a catheter. I was really hoping to find him connected to life supporting machinery that I could simply unplug, but I had come to realise that murdering somebody isn't always going to be as easy as you first anticipate. I turned the monitor off at the wall anyway – no point in letting the alarm trigger, sending in all the real doctors when his heart stopped beating.

I pulled a pillow out from underneath his head, and it thudded back down onto the mattress. His eyes flew open.

Whether they opened because he woke up, or whether it was the bounce back from his head hitting the bed, I didn't wait to find out. I took a huge preparatory gulp of air and slammed the pillow over his nose and mouth. At first it did not seem that he was fighting it. Maybe he could breathe perfectly fine under there, or maybe he would slip easily into death, but after a few moments, his body began convulsing. His legs and arms started twitching, each spasm getting more and more violent, throwing the blankets up into a twisted heap and tugging at the tubes that connected him to the monitor. Even unconscious he was almost overpoweringly strong; it took all of my might to hold the pillow down over his airways. The blood in my blackened eyes and broken nose throbbed painfully and sweat splashed down my face onto the pillow. My arms were aching, they were so heavy, he was so heavy. His whole torso was shaking, rattling the bed. I wouldn't be able to keep this up for much longer. The dizziness was coming, the room was getting darker, my vision closed in around him and I felt lightheaded…

And then he stopped moving.

Finally.

I let my muscles relax and my arms sagged on top of the pillow, the room flooding back to me.

I had finally done it.

There was a clinking noise, from outside. I froze to the spot, as the shard of light from the corridor fell, once more, upon his torso.

I threw the pillow onto the chair behind me. Rob lay there with his blank, bloodshot eyes wide open, staring at the ceiling, his mouth lopsided. The light grew bigger, something rattled, a wheel squeaked, and a person was walking into the room, arse first, dragging a trolley behind them.

Behind her. A nurse, in a dark blue tunic. My mind was

completely blank. I had no plan, no explanation. The nurse continued to wiggle into the room; she seemed preoccupied with something on the trolley, something jangly, medicine maybe. This was my chance to do something. But what? Knock the nurse out of the way and run? Jump out of the window? Hide in the bathroom?

Too late – she had turned around.

"Fuck!" she yelped, clutching at her heart when she saw me standing there.

We stared at each other for what felt like forever.

"You?" she said.

Ella Richie stepped forward into the path of what little moonlight shone in through the window. She tucked a strand of long blonde hair behind her ear and glanced at Rob; his eyes stared into oblivion, his blankets were heaped around his waist and his hairy legs poked out the bottom of his gown.

"Is he dead?" she asked impassively.

I nodded.

She calmly took the pillow from the armchair, unceremoniously pushed his head up and stuffed it back underneath. She began to straighten his blankets. "Go," she muttered to me.

I did not need to be told twice. I threw Ella a look that I hoped was halfway between a thank you and an apology, and speed-walked out of the room and down the corridor.

When I reached the entrance to the ward soundless flashing red lights bombarded the passageway.

"Doctor! He's having a cardiac arrest!" screamed Ella from a distance.

I slammed my hand against the green exit button and began to march quickly, but not too quickly, away from the ward. This time the adrenaline was catching up with me a lot sooner; it pretty much carried down the stairs and back out through to the main reception, hammering my heart hard against my ribs. I dropped the ring binder back into the metal tray on my way past, sincerely hoping that I had not left any fingerprints on it.

In the car I allowed my breathing to return to almost normal before driving off. I felt like I couldn't go straight home, or maybe that I didn't want to go straight home. I felt tainted, icky, and I seriously needed some sugar. So I drove to the 24-hour Tesco that I'd vowed I would never return to.

At that time of night, I had a plethora of parking spaces to choose from, but again I decided to park away from the entrance. The mess from the BMW was all cleared up. I wondered what had happened to Clive's golf clubs? Neither the security guards at the front, nor any of the staff members seemed to recognise me from Friday.

Good.

I bought a pint of Ben and Jerry's and a pack of plastic picnic cutlery and ate the whole thing in Olly's car in the dark. I watched the rats jumping in and out of the privet bushes and tried to summon an emotion. Tried, and failed. Nothing would happen, not a smile or a single tear. Maybe I was dead inside?

Oliver was not asleep when I got home. He had brought the travel cot into the master bedroom and was lying awake on the bed, fully-clothed, with the curtains wide open. He jumped to his feet when he saw me.

"I'm sorry that I took your car, she's OK," I whispered.

Oliver swept me into his arms. "I don't give a fuck about the car, I'm just so glad you're safe." He tightened his grip, blood pulsated through my forehead and broken nose. "So?"

"So what? Did I kill him? Yeah, I did."

"Fuck!" He was laughing and kissing any and every bit of me that he could. "You're a fucking badass!"

I laughed too; it hurt my face, but it felt so good. "Yeah, I am a fucking badass."

The next morning I woke up to the smell of bacon frying. I jumped out of bed; my head was excruciating. I looked in on the travel cot, but it was empty.

"Good morning my little killer queen," said Oliver with a smile when I got to the kitchen. He was holding a spatula in one hand and a baby bottle in the other.

I frowned at the bottle. "What's in that?"

"Formula," said Olly. "I had to get some when you were out because she was hungry, and I used up all the frozen breastmilk. Is that OK?" He looked worried, that he might be upsetting the murderer.

I squished my boobs with my hands. I hadn't really thought about it – I guess I'd been too preoccupied – but I hadn't really breastfed or expressed in at least a couple of days. My boobs were big and full, though not the painful engorged rocks I had come to know.

"I wonder if my supply has dropped off now," I said. "I don't know if I can build it back up." I felt deflated. Another thing about committing murder that people don't bother to mention; it dries up your milk supply. Had I failed as a mother?

"Are you going to work today?" asked Oliver, as he handed me a bacon bap, oozing with brown sauce.

"I suppose," I sighed. "I don't want to give Clive any excuse to fire me, can't really afford thirty grand right now."

. . .

Work was, predictably, unbearable. Clive made to mention several times how I could not just call in sick on a whim because I had embarrassed myself in front of the entire payroll and didn't want to face the consequences or some shit like that, though thankfully made no mention of any further disciplinaries. Three times he had asked me where his clubs were, and three times I successfully deflected the subject, mentioning my training schedule and something about a tribunal.

Ryan made jokes about my black eyes, asking who I'd pissed off this time, and loudly declaring that he'd like to take them out for a beer, while repeatedly repositioning his Lawyer of the Year award. I placated myself with the simple fact that I was a cold-blooded murderer, and should I ever daydream about taking down Clive or Ryan, then at least there would be some gravitas to it.

Niamh was consolatory, but maybe slightly distant? Disappointed with me? I know that she would have loved nothing more than to walk away from this place, with two fingers held high. She printed off a countdown calendar of my days left at Caine Reynolds and made me pinky-promise that I would hand my notice in the moment the counter hit zero. She confessed that the previous Friday she'd had an interview at a rival firm. She said it hadn't gone too well and wasn't expecting anything from it, but there was a clawing feeling in the pit of my stomach that I couldn't ignore; this new company solely practiced family law, so there would be no way I could join her if she did leave. I didn't have the experience, though I'd probably proven to myself I had the emotional resolve, even if I couldn't tell anyone.

Lauren and the other admin staff were slowly beginning to talk to me again. Since I no longer needed anywhere to express at work, I wasn't often over that end of the office, but I hated the thought that they were still mad at me. That is until one time, when I popped in to do some photocopying for Ryan and I caught Lauren regaling some of the other staff with tales of my resignation speech, and how it all seemed so funny in retrospect. I still continued to make them cappuccinos every time I went to the other side of the building. It was my feeble attempt at an apology.

Then on Friday morning a letter arrived from the District Judge Magistrate's court. I was being summoned. For contravening the Criminal Damage Act 1971 by vandalising a vehicle with the license plate L4ND3D, and I must attend court on Wednesday 1st April to answer the complaint. *Wonder how much this will cost me?*

I hadn't yet heard from the police regarding the man I'd suffocated. I honestly didn't know what to think or feel about all of this. I was completely numb. My only real regret, of all the crimes I'd committed in those last few days, was that I didn't actually help the mom with the oranges; I just left all her fruit all over the car park, for some reason that left a lead weight in my stomach. And Marie, she still hadn't said much to any of us.

I guessed that in the coming days or weeks it would begin to dawn on me, and I would start to feel something. Remorse maybe? I'd killed a man. I caused criminal damage to a – mostly innocent – man's car. I put myself and my friends – not to mention their babies – in serious jeopardy.

I didn't move the travel cot from our bedroom. Every night I curled up on the bed and just gazed at River in the moonlight. She was so peaceful. She had no idea what I'd done. I wondered if I would ever tell her. I didn't sleep for the rest of the week, I don't think. Oliver whinged every time River stirred in the night and I jumped up to nuzzle her into my breast, but he wouldn't sleep downstairs like I told him to.

The weekend arrived and with it my very first Mother's Day. Olly brought a tray bearing toast and coffee up to bed in the morning. He had also bought me flowers, and a gift certificate for a nearby spa, with the promise that his mom would have River one weekend.

He kissed me. "You deserve it babe, I honestly never appreciated everything you do for us before. I especially never expected you to kill for us."

"I did it for River. And Marie. I still can't believe you're OK with that though," I said, and sipped my coffee.

Except that it was never for Marie. Even at the very beginning, it was always for me. I wanted to be the hero, I wanted to be helping the needy. But Marie was never needy, she never asked any of us to step in – everything she said was always matter-of-fact. I had been doing it for myself. All along.

Ding-dong.

The doorbell. Who would be calling this early on Mother's Day? *Please don't be Colleen.* I groaned.

Oliver jumped up. "I'll get it."

I shuffled to the end of the bed to better hear who it was.

Seconds later Oliver called out. "Jaime." He had his serious voice on. "There's someone here to see you."

Fuck it's the police.

I toyed with the idea of getting dressed before going downstairs. If I was going to be arrested, on Mother's Day of all days, I'd at least like to look nice. Instead I threw on my dressing gown and trundled down the stairs. My heart began to palpitate. Too much caffeine? Oliver always made the coffee too strong. I needed to brush my teeth; I didn't want to go to prison with stinking breath.

It wasn't the police, however. Sitting in the centre of my grey sofa, was a brown-haired woman wearing a baby in a red carrier on her chest.

"I got the train, and then a taxi from the station. I hope you don't mind."

"Hi, Marie. Oh my gosh, how are you?" I rushed forward and gave Marie Sparks a hug, sandwiching her baby between us.

"You look like I did two weeks ago," she said, gazing at my face, but then instantly looking away. "I just came to see you and...say...thank you. For freeing me." It was barely above a whisper.

"Oh, well, you're more than welcome," I said, surprised, "my pleasure really," and we began laughing. And then I found it so strange that we were two women, one a widow, and the other a murderer, laughing about the death of her husband, that I laughed even more. And then we were laughing about that, and we couldn't stop, until we were wiping tears from our eyes and clutching the stitches in our sides. She lifted her baby out of the carrier and set her down on the carpet next to River.

"So you're not mad with me, for murdering your husband?" My heartbeat throbbed behind my eyes and broken nose. I held my breathe while waiting for her answer.

Her smile remained on her lips, but her eyes dropped. She looked at her hands.

I had an urge to apologise, but I couldn't bring myself to do it. It would be a downright lie. Like Kelly said, she's better without him, but whether she'd ever realise that was another thing.

"Can I get you a drink?" I said instead.

"Oliver's making some tea I think."

"I'M ON IT!" he yelled from the kitchen.

"It sucks about your work huh?" said Marie. I guess she wanted to change the subject, but there were still things I needed to know.

"Yeah," I pulled a pouty face. "Only fifty days left before I can sack it off though. Have you heard from the police or anyone?" I tried to make it sound offhand.

"Yes actually, I have."

My stomach dropped; I took a sharp intake of breath.

"The coroner has apparently ruled Rob's death as pulmonary embolism, whatever that means, and they think it's incidental to the hit and run. They think the hit and run killed him basically."

"They did an autopsy?"

She nodded.

"And this is the conclusion they came to?"

She nodded again. "They said that it may have been a targeted attack, or just an accident. They asked me if he has any enemies, and I said yes, many, but they know that it can't be me because I was in the safe house in Lincoln. I didn't tell them about Ella. I don't know if Bradley will."

"She wasn't involved though," I said, thinking back to the night in the hospital. This wasn't entirely true.

"She's a nurse at Queen Elizabeth. I think she was on shift at the time of the hit and run anyway."

I bit my lip. When I retold the events of that evening to the group, I neglected to mention that Ella was there. I didn't want to get her into trouble. If anybody was going to take the fall for this, it would be me. After all, she wasn't the one that suffocated her fiancé to death. "I guess we just wait then," I said.

"The police said that they are still looking for the vehicle or vehicles involved, but unless any new evidence arises, they don't have much to go on. So, I'm not sure they are going to investigate it too much. It kinda feels like they've given up looking for the bus."

"That suits me fine," I said. "Hopefully they never find it, or us."

I didn't know why I was being so calm about it all really, only that if the police found me there wouldn't be much I could do about it. Why flap about and get stressed anymore? If I was going to spend eternity in prison at least I could be certain that Olly would do an amazing job of raising River. He'd really stepped up, not that I'd expected anything less from him.

"Um, I wanted to do something for you actually," said Marie in almost a whisper. She picked at the hem on her t-shirt. "A long time ago, just after we got married, Rob was made to take out life insurance for a job he was doing at the time… something on the docks, I think… I forgot that he had it. Well I had a letter yesterday to say that they are going to award me the full pay-out. I wanted to give you—"

I interrupted her. "I can't possibly take any money from you."

Marie put her hand onto my arm. "You have no choice. I'm going to pay off your maternity leave, so that you don't have to go back to that horrible place, and I want you to take enough money so that you can start your company, with your friend, the Irish one."

I opened my mouth to speak, but no words came. Tears were streaming down my face and splashing onto my dressing gown. Eventually I said, "It'll be a loan? I'll pay you back."

"Sure," said Marie, who was crying too.

We hugged, for at least a whole minute. Oliver came into the room with three cups of tea.

"Just out of interest, how much was the policy worth?" I asked, curious to know that I wasn't about to rob my friend of her entire fortune. I gulped my tea.

"Four hundred and eighty thousand pounds!" she squealed.

I spat the tea back into my cup.

"I'm going to give some to Ella too, I think it's only fair. And some to the other mums from the group. You've always been there for me. Always."

"What are you going to do with the rest?" said Oliver, over the top of his cup.

She shrugged. "Pay off the mortgage. Take Daisy on her first holiday maybe." She sipped her tea. "Ooh, call your friend, and tell her please. Tell her that you can quit your job and start your own company." Her eyes lit up.

I watched her face for a few moments, she looked excited, and happy. Who am I to rob her of this moment? "OK, let me just go and get my phone. I left it upstairs."

Oliver said nothing, he held out his arm and handed me his phone. I found Niamh's number and pressed the green call button.

"Hello? Olly? Is Jaime OK?" she said.

"Hi Niamh, it's me, I'm just using Olly's phone."

"Hun, what's wrong?" She sounded concerned.

"Nothing, actually, everything is great. I've got some news." I told her that Marie was there with me and that she was going to pay back my maternity pay, and loan us enough money to start a practice together.

Niamh was silent for what felt like minutes. Finally, she

screamed, "Hun! That's brilliant! I'm going to hand my notice in tomorrow." Her voice was shaking. "We've got so much to do: find premises, apply for authorisation, decide what kind of company we want to form... Oh my gosh. What should we do first?"

I didn't need to think about it, I said, "Can we go desk shopping?"

Erin Schellenger - 23rd March - 11:30

Morning everyone, hope you all had lovely Mother's Days. So we said before that if we were going to have any new members we would have to take a vote on it. Well, I can tell you that we all voted unanimously, and I'd like to introduce you all to our newest member, Ella Ritchie. Welcome Ella.

Ella Ritchie - 23rd March - 11:35

Thank you guys for letting me join. I'm looking forward to getting to know you all and your babies. For anyone wondering, I'm currently 13+1, and baby's due 24th September.

ABOUT THE AUTHOR

Nina lives in sunny grey Bristol, with her husband, two young daughters, and two butthead griffon bruxellllois. She enjoys foods with unnaturally high sugar content, camping in her 1986 VW T25 bus, and watching excessive amounts of YouTube videos.

Full Mama Bear is book one in the Hitmums series and Nina's first published work. She is currently writing the second in the series, which will be available soon.

If you enjoyed Full Mamabear and want to know about new releases, please follow Nina on social media:

On Instagram @ninamwilde
   And Facebook @fullmamabear

Or go to www.ninamwilde.com to sign up for the newsletter, where you can receive free content and learn about new releases.

ALSO BY THE AUTHOR

**Pipistrelle
Hitmums Book Two
Coming Soon**

Visually impaired mum of three, Molly Cheung, is addicted to true crime fiction, and she's convinced she knows exactly how to pull off the perfect murder and get away with it scot-free.

Trouble is, she'll never get a chance to prove it.

Until, one day, an opportune contract falls neatly into her lap: kill taxi driver, Wickley Curry, at the South West Crime Literature Festival, make it look like an accident and collect a twenty grand payout.

Simple right?

Will Molly be able to teach herself assassination 101 and

finish the job before the end of the festival? And more importantly, will she get away with it?